THE QUEEN'S MAN

REGENCY ROYALS BOOK 5

JESS MICHAELS

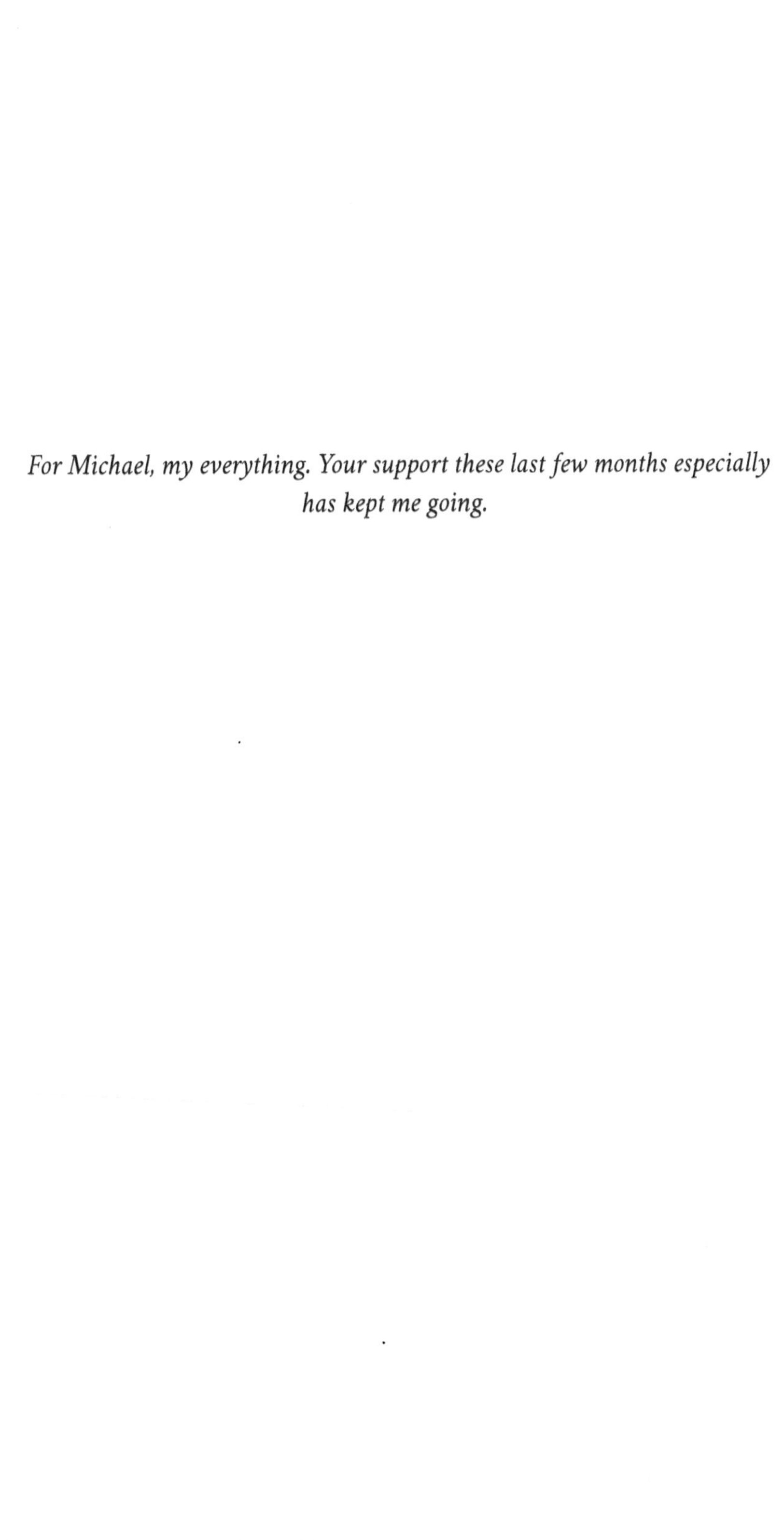

For Michael, my everything. Your support these last few months especially has kept me going.

PROLOGUE

1816

Dashiell Talbot had worked for Giabella, Queen of Athawick, for almost ten years when her husband died. It had been a long illness, the end was expected, but that did not make it any easier to stand outside her chamber door at four in the morning, waiting to knock. To wake her. To give her this news.

The problem, of course, was that Dash was in love with her.

He had been since even before she had asked him to join her staff as her personal secretary. Since the first moment he saw her, if one wanted to be specific. He could recall every moment of that day when he brought the child of a member of court to be presented to her after the girl was orphaned. Giabella had taken her in. That was more than fifteen years prior.

Loving Gia had been the greatest joy and the deepest heartache of his life, because, of course, it could come to nothing.

He cleared his throat and knocked. There was hesitation from within and then the bustling of the queen's maid. Giabella had always been an early riser, so Betsy was in her room by four every day in order to light the fires and ready the gowns and do all the things a queen needed done before she rose from bed at six to start her official day.

Betsy cracked the door, and when she saw Dash there, her eyes widened. Her gaze flitted to the black armband he now wore and she nodded slightly.

"I'll wake her, sir," she said softly.

He followed her into the sitting room and looked around. The curtains had not been pulled open yet so the room was lit only by the fire. A haunting glow that danced off all the personal items that said so much about the queen. Portraits of her beloved children, including Grantham, who for the last half hour had been king. A painting by one of her dearest friends hung on the wall, an artist she had championed for years. A pair of her slippers was tucked partly beneath the settee. He smiled as he pictured her sliding them off before she folded into herself and read on the couch the previous night before she retired to bed.

Betsy reappeared from the bedchamber and nodded. "She's ready, sir."

He entered the bedroom. Normally a man like him, unmarried to a lady, would never see the intimacy of her bedchamber. But he was a servant, her most trusted one, and he knew he was seen as almost sexless. At least by others. Occasionally Gia would look at him and he felt...

No, it was wrong to consider that now. Today of all days.

Giabella was propped up on her pillows, her hair arranged around her shoulders. She was still in her nightrail and he swallowed hard at how utterly lovely she was. Her dark hair was just barely touched by gray at the temples, her face expressive. Today it was pensive. She already knew what he would say.

He reached back and shut the door to the chamber. Inappropriate, perhaps, but no one else needed to hear her response when he gave her this news.

"Your Majesty," he began softly.

"He is dead, isn't he?"

Slowly, Dash inclined his head. "He is. I am so very sorry."

She held his gaze a moment before she pushed the covers back and paced across the room to the window. She threw open the curtain and the pinks and purples of sunrise hit her, outlining her body beneath the thin nightgown. He ducked his head, tried not to look as he fetched her robe. He placed it over her shoulders gently and she turned toward him.

They were close now, probably too close, and she stared up at him. Her dark brown eyes sparkled with tears, her hands shook as she reached out and caught one of his lapels in her fist.

"How can I...how can I *hate* him so much and yet feel such a deep pain at his passing?" she whimpered.

He ignored propriety and wrapped his arms around her, drawing her to his chest. She shuddered against him, her arms coming around his waist and holding tight, like he was the only solid thing keeping her from washing out into the sea that sparkled in the distance.

"Your marriage was..." He shook his head. "Complicated. Of course your feelings would be, as well."

She nodded against his chest and then sighed. "Does Grantham know?"

"Yes. And Remi. He was with his father at the end."

"Poor Remi," Giabella breathed. "The girls will have to be told, too. Though perhaps we should wait until a more reasonable hour."

"I agree," he said. "No use waking them. There is nothing they can do."

She lifted her face toward his, drawing a short breath as if to say something more. She didn't. It was as if she had just realized the precarious and inappropriate nature of their position. He released her immediately, but she didn't move, didn't make any attempt to step away. She just kept staring at him.

God help him, he wanted to kiss her. It wasn't the first time he'd felt it, but definitely the worst in this moment when her pain and heartbreak and worry was so clear on every line of her face. Her hands shook against him, tears threatened to fall even as she focused so intently on his lips that he was shocked to realize she might want the same thing. As comfort? As relief?

He had no idea, but he shivered as she lifted up a little, closer to him. He felt the broken stir of her breath against his lips, and every part of him reacted exactly as it shouldn't.

He bent his head as he backed away, extracting himself from her embrace with more difficulty than he had ever done anything before. Her cheeks brightened with embarrassment and she faced the sea again.

"I will dress and go see the princes..." Her breath shuddered out. "I'm sorry, Remi and the king. Grantham is king now."

"Long live the king," Dash said softly.

She faced him and she had erased whatever longing had been there a moment ago. She was Queen Giabella again, proper and elegant and wonderful.

"Long live the king," she repeated.

He executed a bow. "I will wait for you outside. And after you have met with him, I will join the gathering of his courtiers and create a schedule for the announcements, as well as the funeral and other official ceremonies."

She sighed. "It will be a very busy time, I fear."

"And I will make it as easy as I can for you."

She smiled slightly. "You always have. Thank you, Dash."

He tensed at her use of his nickname. She so rarely used it that every time she did it felt like her nails raking along his back. He bowed again and backed from the room, motioning for her maid to go ready her for greeting the new king as Dash stepped into the hall to wait for her.

As he had been waiting for her for years. As he would wait for her until his last breath.

CHAPTER 1

It had been almost eighteen months since the death of her husband, and in that time, Giabella, Queen Mother of Athawick, had spoken or written about almost every moment of that day. Save one.

That was the moment she had nearly kissed her longtime secretary, Dashiell Talbot.

That moment she had *never* mentioned, not to her children, not to a confidante, not to the man himself. Dash had done the same, politely pretending she hadn't almost humiliated herself in that awful moment where relief and grief and anxiety had mixed in her chest, making the future blurred.

"What do you think of this one, Mama?"

Giabella lifted her gaze, her attention drawn back to the two women across the room from her. Her daughters-in-law, Priscilla and Ophelia, princess and queen respectively. But she felt as close to them as she did her real daughters, Ilaria and Sasha.

She moved toward them with a smile that was only slightly forced. They had all been looking at fabrics for an upcoming ball and now Ophelia held up a swath of blue silk that almost perfectly matched the Athawickian flag. A purposeful choice and one that made Giabella smile.

"It's lovely and it will make your eyes pop," she said.

Priscilla laughed and nudged Ophelia. "Which is exactly the effect she wishes to have on the people. And her husband."

Giabella laughed along with them as she watched the two women. She had been very lucky in the matches all her children had made. Ilaria and Sasha had married Englishmen and were in London living what sounded like wonderful lives, according to their letters. They would soon return to the island and then…well, then everything would change.

"The election is so close now, and the dissolution of the Crown as soon as the results are tabulated," Giabella said softly. "How is Grantham doing?"

Some of the glee went out of Ophelia's eyes. "He is somber but hopeful, I think. He has come to terms with the fact that he will give up his royal title, that he will no longer be king. And he seems excited about the idea that he will likely win the election and have the opportunity to marshal his people into a new era."

Giabella nodded. She was so proud of her son, who cared so deeply for his country that he would give up his power over it. And most shared in that pride and happiness. The few who didn't?

Well, they were troublesome, but Giabella hoped not dangerous. All she could do was stand behind Grantham, support him in every way he needed. Which was frankly not much now that he had Ophelia to lean upon.

She tried not to ponder that overly much as there was a light knock on the door behind them. She turned, and she and Ophelia spoke at the same time. "Come in."

They met each other's gaze and laughed softly. Two queens in a palace often led to many an awkward exchange. The door to the parlor opened and Giabella's laughter faded as Dashiell Talbot entered.

Her heart skipped a beat even though she didn't wish it to. But then again, it had been skipping a beat for every moment she'd spent with him over the last fifteen years. He was such a handsome man, with brown hair that was touched with gray. He was tall and broad shouldered, with dark blue eyes that had always reminded her of sapphires. At present he had a neatly trimmed beard that only served to accentuate a very nice set of lips.

She shivered as she dropped her gaze away from said lips and forced a smile to her own. "Dashiell," she said. "Am I needed?"

There was a brief moment where his pupils dilated ever so slightly but then the reaction was gone, erased as he always erased anything improper.

"Your Majesty. The king would like to see you," he said, obviously addressing Giabella rather than Ophelia. "*Us*, actually."

She wrinkled her brow and glanced at her daughters-in-law, then back to Dash. "Of course. Ladies, all the fabrics you've chosen are divine. There is not a wrong option in the bunch."

Ophelia and Priscilla smiled at her before they returned to their sorting of the materials. Giabella drew a breath before she stepped toward Dash. He always smelled good, an intoxicating blend of woods and mint and *him*. She reined in the urge to take a long breath of him as he held out a hand to allow her to exit the room first, as was proper.

She slowed her steps so he could catch up with her and they walked together up the hallway. Behind them there was a peal of giggles from Priscilla and Ophelia, and Giabella smiled up at him. "My sons have made excellent matches. And my daughters, as well."

"Indeed, that is true. The last few months have been a whirlwind and I'm sure the next will be little better...but it is good to remember that there is still a great amount of joy to be found amidst the chaos."

She nodded but didn't reply. She couldn't think of anything appropriate to say, in truth. Joy in chaos. She'd never had much of that personally. Only pain with glimpses of light that almost always came from her current companion.

She glanced down at their hands, so close as they walked. She could almost slide her fingers into his. She could almost touch him. But she didn't, of course. She never did.

They reached the study and Dash took the lead, cracking the door and inclining his head. "Your Majesty? I've found the queen."

"Please enter," Grantham's voice rumbled behind the door.

Dash stepped out of the way again and she moved into the room first. Her eldest was on his feet already, making his way around the huge desk so he could press a kiss to her cheek. "Good morning, Mama. I'm sorry I missed you at breakfast."

"You have a great deal to do," she said. "I'm happy to see you whenever you have a moment." She glanced at the piles of papers and reports spread across Grantham's desk. "Everything is well?"

"It is…getting there," Grantham said with a sigh. He motioned to the chairs across from his desk. "Please sit, both of you."

Dash hesitated but did join her. This wasn't entirely unheard of. The children had always embraced Dash as part of the family, and that had only increased since the death of the previous king. "What can I help with, Your Majesty?" Dash asked.

Giabella glanced toward him with a grateful smile. Although he had been her secretary for years, he had recently been assisting Grantham after the underhanded plotting of some of his highest-ranking courtiers had been revealed. That meant she saw Dash a little less, unfortunately, but it was all for a good cause. At least that was what she told herself when she turned and didn't find him there as she had always found him there for so long.

"As you are both well aware, the election will be in just a month," Grantham said. "And while every sign says I will win as prime minister and that the transition of power will be reasonably peaceful, there are still a few hesitations here and there."

"Are things dangerous?" Giabella asked softly.

Grantham tilted his head. "I think no more than usual, Mama. But I did have an idea and I wanted to ask for your assistance."

Giabella leaned forward. Since Grantham's marriage, Ophelia

had taken over a great many duties as queen. She was always open to Giabella's opinion and presence, of course, but life had certainly shifted these past few months. The opportunity to actually *do* something was very exciting.

"Anything," she said.

"Would you be willing to do a small tour of the island, specifically the Southern Realm? Jonah has been in London and hasn't been able to make his presence as count known, so it is the most restless part of the country at present. But you are so very loved by our people—I think seeing you would shore things up a bit."

Giabella nodded. "Whatever you need, my love. I haven't been able to travel the island since before your father's death. I would look forward to seeing some of the country and people, especially if it would help you."

"And I know that I have occupied Dash's time of late, but obviously he would accompany you," Grantham continued.

Giabella glanced at Dash from the corner of her eye and was surprised to see him flinch ever so slightly at the suggestion. She forced her gaze back to Grantham and used decades of practice to keep the hurt at that reaction from her face. "When would you like for me to go?" she asked.

"A few days?" Grantham suggested. "Count Hadley and Count Friskar, as well as some of the others, will be in the area by week's end, and since Hadley is not entirely supportive of this election—"

"Hateful man," Giabella breathed, and couldn't help but look at Dash. He had touched his arm, at the place he'd been shot months ago while trying to protect Grantham.

"Indeed," Grantham agreed. "But since we could never prove his complacency in the plot to harm our family, he is a necessary evil, I'm afraid. And I thought the gathering might be the perfect place to show him the support is on our side."

"Of course." Giabella rose. "I will go up right away and start my preparations. Excuse me."

Grantham wrinkled his brow at her sudden departure, but rose to his feet as she did. "Of course. Thank you, Mama. I could not do this without the family's full-throated support. I appreciate it and you more than I could ever say."

She squeezed his hand, sent a sideways look to Dash and then left the room. As she shut the door behind herself, she hesitated. In all his years of service, she had never seen Dash unhappy to do something on her behalf. But everything was changing. Perhaps he didn't wish to *be* at her side any longer. An idea that crushed her. Crushed her more deeply than she should have allowed.

So she pushed aside the feeling and walked away. But the uneasiness was not so easy to erase. She feared it never would be.

Dash watched as Giabella slipped from the room, his heart sinking. There had been such tension when she looked at him. Not the usual kind, the push and pull between desire and duty…but something darker. More painful.

"Have you told her?"

He jumped at Grantham's voice intruding upon his thoughts. Slowly he faced his king. "Er…no, not yet."

"I'm surprised to hear that. Is there reason for your hesitation?" Grantham tilted his head.

Dash took a long breath. There was no way he could get into the plethora of reasons for his hesitations in telling Giabella that her son had offered him a full-time position in the government if the election came out in his favor. Not a servant's place, but a place at the larger table, helping to steer the nation into its new future. And that he was strongly considering it.

Why?

Well, because being near the queen had become increasingly difficult in the last year and a half as she navigated the waters of widowhood. As her looks in his direction became longer. As memories of that night he'd nearly kissed her grew larger and louder and more insistent. One day he knew he would not be able to resist touching her…and then the world would change. Probably not for the better.

"Dash?"

He shook his head. "She has faced so much change since the death of King Alistair. This will—" He stopped himself. He had no right to suggest he held an importance in her life. Even if he knew it was true. "I *will* speak to her, Your Majesty. Perhaps there will be a good moment on this trip. After we feel out what is happening in the south and with the aristocracy."

Grantham stared at him evenly, his expression unreadable as it was often unreadable. He drummed his fingers against the desktop. "I simply don't want to see her hurt because I care for her. As I know you do."

Dash swallowed and dropped his gaze. "Of course. As you said, all her subjects hold Queen Giabella in the utmost—"

"Dash," Grantham interrupted softly. "I know you care for her."

"Will that be all, Your Majesty?" Dashiell pushed to his feet and Grantham followed, still watching him impassively.

"Yes. All the arrangements should be swiftly made now that you are serving both her office and mine. Good day."

Dash bowed and then moved to the door. As he stepped out in the hallway, he flexed his hand, trying to put blood back into his fingers. None of Giabella's children, even Sasha, who Dash considered as almost his own daughter, had ever seemed to notice his attachment to Giabella.

Was he so weak that he was letting the walls come down? Yet another reason to separate himself before he did damage to her. To himself.

He moved down the hall at a focused clip, trying to make his mind go back to more appropriate topics. But he had not gone very far when Giabella stepped out of a parlor he had just passed. "Dashiell?"

He stopped, frozen at the sound of his name from her lips. He smoothed his jacket and slowly turned to face her. "Your Majesty, I did not realize you were still downstairs. I thought you had gone up to your quarters to have your maids ready your wardrobe."

She stepped into the hallway and closed half the distance between them. "I was going to do so, but I…I wanted to speak to you, so I waited here."

He blinked. "Speak to me?"

She motioned him toward the parlor. "Will you join me?"

He nodded and entered the room. When he turned, he watched her shut the door behind her and rest her hand against the barrier for a moment too long. They were alone. And they were often alone, yet this time felt different somehow. More charged.

She faced him and worried her hands before her. "Have I…done something to upset you?"

He moved toward her almost against his will. "Of course not! Why would you think such a thing?"

"I could see your resistance to attending me on this trip," she said softly. "Do you not wish to go?"

"I am happy to go," he assured her. "If you saw resistance it is only because of my concerns about your safety. You know I begin to run those equations the moment a new plan is hatched."

She nodded, but there was no mistaking her relief in his answers. It washed over her beautiful face like a waterfall. "Oh good," she breathed, raising a hand to her heart. "For you know I cannot do without you."

He took another step in her direction and now they were certainly too close. He flexed his fingers but didn't touch her. An impossible task. "Of course you could. You have always been more than capable at everything you've ever done, Gia…" He stopped as she caught her breath. "Your Majesty," he corrected himself.

"Dash," she whispered, her voice barely carrying in the slim space between them. He saw her body coil, ready to move even closer. To go beyond too close. To unleash something he would have to physically fight to deny himself.

But before control could be lost, there was a knock on the parlor door. She jumped and stepped back before she said, "Yes?"

When the door opened, it was Giabella's maid, Betsy, who stood there. Her gaze darted from the queen to Dash and back. "I'm sorry to interrupt, Your Majesty, sir, but I've been informed of the imminent travel plans and I have asked that the royal tiaras and crowns be brought for you to choose from if you have time."

Giabella shot Dash a quick glance before she turned to the door. "Yes, of course. I know we have little opportunity to ready for this journey so let us get that out of the way." She stopped and looked back over her shoulder. "Dashiell."

"Your Majesty," he said softly.

She left then, Betsy trailing after her, the two of them chattering about gowns and crowns. He sagged, gripping the back of the closest chair.

He didn't know why, but this...this thing between them had suddenly veered into the realm of impossible. And he would have to find a way to fight that or else risk destroying his future, along with that of the woman he so desperately loved.

CHAPTER 2

Giabella motioned to one of the trunks lined up in her antechamber. "I think take both," she said to Betsy, who was holding up two gowns. "They each match the jewels and we will decide what is best once I arrive and feel out the situation more fully."

"As you wish, Your Majesty," Betsy said, and motioned to the other maids, who carefully began to fold the gowns.

Giabella sighed as she moved to the table to look at the shoes her maid had lined up. She pulled pairs forward, indicating which she wished to take. This had been her life for the last few days, this ceaseless choosing and planning and imagining what impact she would make with a ring or a gown. It wasn't that she didn't understand the truth of that fact. This was her armor, after all; she was entering what could be enemy territory.

It was just that she was so tired of all of it. So wrung out after years of this performative dance.

There was a knock at her chamber door and she pivoted to face it, heart leaping. Dash had been so busy doing his own preparations that she had seen very little of him since their last encounter in the parlor. The one she'd kept reliving over and over, analyzing his every facial expression and glance.

Now she found herself holding her breath as Betsy opened the door to reveal if it was the man himself. Breath she expelled as Remi, her younger son, entered the chamber instead.

"Oh, Mama, you look so disappointed to see me," he teased as he stepped around the trunks and piles and made his way to kiss her cheek.

She swatted his arm lightly. "Of course I am not. I am always overjoyed to see you, as you well know."

"Because I'm your favorite," he drawled with a wink.

She rolled her eyes but didn't correct him. She loved all her children, but Remi wasn't wrong. His brightness made it impossible not to adore him. She always had and she always would.

"Are you here to torment your poor mother or is something else on your mind?" she asked, going back to sorting her slippers.

Remi stepped up next to her and pushed a pair of the shoes back, replacing it with another. When she arched her brow at him, he shrugged. "The peach are prettier and you've told me before that they are also more comfortable." She left his selection and he laughed. "So, it seems you are nearly ready for Grantham's pony show."

She shot him a look. "Now, now. I am happy to do this for him. We all do our part in this family."

He cocked his head, and suddenly her playful son's expression became a little more serious. "We all make sacrifices?"

She pursed her lips. There was clearly an undercurrent to the question. And judging from the way the maids were all side-eyeing them, they heard it too. She pivoted and smiled at the small group of women. "May we have the room a moment?"

"Of course, Your Majesty," Betsy said with a meaningful look to the others. The rest curtseyed as they all began to leave the room.

Once they were alone, Giabella speared Remi with a glance. "I thought you and Grantham were getting along better."

Remi's eyes went wide. "We are, Mama. Closer than ever, actually. When I spoke of sacrifices, it is only because I have been thinking lately that you have sacrificed more than most."

She stepped away, smoothing her hands over her skirts. "I'm not sure I know what you mean."

He arched a brow at her, his expression making it plain that he didn't believe *that* for a moment. "What will you do when this is over?" he asked.

She blinked. "When the election has been held?"

He nodded. "And Grantham takes on this new role. When we all become simply...*people*. No longer royalty, or at least Athawickian royalty."

She shifted. "I'm not sure," she admitted. "It will be a change, certainly."

"You could do anything."

She worried her lip gently as her mind suddenly turned to thoughts of Dash. "Yes. I suppose I could."

"With anyone," Remi said.

She jerked her gaze back to his and saw a knowing glint in his light blue eyes. "Remington," she said, her tone a warning.

He ignored it and reached out, taking both her hands in his. "All of your children have found love. Please don't give up on it yourself. I know you have—"

She drew in a breath and interrupted, "You needn't worry about me, dearest."

He laughed. "And yet I do." He leaned forward to kiss her forehead. "Do you leave in the morning?"

"Yes," she said. "Very early."

"Then our last supper must be jolly, indeed," he said, and offered her his arm.

She took it with a smile and allowed him to lead her from the chamber and toward the stairs. But his words lingered in her mind, even as they began to chat about far more benign subjects. The idea that she could do anything was one she had not yet fully pondered.

Because when she did, she knew that her fantasies about the future would all involve one man.

~

Dash didn't always join the royal family for supper, but since the death of Giabella's husband, he had become a far more frequent visitor at their table. The formality of their gatherings had decreased as their closeness as a group increased, allowing for it. Actually, a great deal of formality had shifted in the last eighteen months. For example, almost everyone exclusively called him Dash now, including the queen.

Tonight, he watched with a smile as the family chatted and laughed, the couples light and easy and playful with each other. It warmed his heart to see how settled they all were.

Of course, that led him to slide his gaze to where Giabella sat. She was a participant in the family dynamic, but there was something...changed about her. He felt it in the way she shifted in her chair, saw it in her eyes when she glanced down the table at him over and over again, igniting the longing that made his body feel like a coiled spring.

Even if it could never lead to anything.

"Do you know your final itinerary for the trip?" Ophelia asked.

Giabella smiled toward him once more. "Dash is the one in charge of all that. I intend to be surprised."

He snorted out a laugh. "Can anyone actually picture that?" All the children laughed along with him even as Giabella blushed prettily. "Let me see. We leave in the morning and stay at Menington House the first night."

"Oh, Menington!" Remi burst out. He glanced toward his wife, Priscilla. "It's a royal residence along the route and it is splendid. Small and intimate with the most glorious views of the sea. It's heavenly—I cannot wait to take you there. Assuming the state will allow it once the royal residences revert after the election."

Grantham inclined his head. "I don't see why it would be a problem."

Priscilla smiled at Remi adoringly. "And I cannot wait to go. It sounds very romantic."

Dash shifted. Good Lord, it *did* sound romantic. It *was*. And he would be almost completely alone with Giabella there. This entire trip was going to be a lesson in control for him.

"We arrive in Bellsport the next afternoon. There is a reception with the aristocracy that night and then a few days touring the region, meeting with various subjects and interests."

Giabella smiled. "I do look forward to that. It has been so very long since I have been out with our people. This will be a lovely change." The clock on the mantel in the dining room chimed as the footmen drew away the last of their plates. Giabella shook her head. "Because we are going so early in the morning, I think I must retire early."

Dash nodded. "I should do the same."

She met his gaze. "Perhaps you could escort me. I have something I wish to discuss with you."

He swallowed hard. "Of course."

The entire party stood and there were warm goodbyes all around since the others would likely not be up so early to see them off. When it was finished, Dash followed Giabella out of the chamber and up the stairs. They turned toward her private quarters and he could hear his heart rate increasing with every step.

They stopped at her door and she worried her hands before her. She was normally so certain of herself, so able to detach herself to perform her duties as need be. But in this moment, she was so very human. So very fragile and precious that he wanted to tuck her into his arms and protect her from everything in the world that could ever hurt her.

"Dashiell," she said at last, looking up at him. Her dark eyes were soft and swept down to his lips and back to his eyes quickly.

"Yes, Your Majesty?" he whispered.

She swallowed. "Dash," she said, this time softer.

He closed his eyes. They never should have crossed the line where she called him Dash for the first time. And yet every time she did it, it was like she lit a match to his desire. Like she beckoned him into a dark corner where they could let what they wanted rule.

And for a moment, he allowed it. "Yes, Gia?"

He heard the break in his voice, the waver of control. She could certainly hear it too. She was no fool.

He opened his eyes and found her staring up at him, lips parted, trembling. She reached for him and then stopped. Hesitated. Then she dropped her gaze. The moment passed.

"I look forward to this time we'll be traveling together. I'll see you in the morning."

She opened her door and sent him a quick glance before she slipped inside and closed him out. He set his hand against the barrier, almost feeling the pulse of her behind it.

"Good night," he murmured before he turned back toward the stairs that led to the servant quarters. Away from her. At least for now. Tomorrow was another story. It remained to be seen what would happen then.

CHAPTER 3

Birds were just beginning to sing as the sun rose along the edge of the sea the next morning. Giabella stepped from the palace and onto the drive where the royal carriage was awaiting her, and took it all in. There was nothing more beautiful in the world than an Athawick morning and nothing more perfect than this very view. She enjoyed it a moment before she let her gaze settle on the rig that would ferry her on this important mission. Alongside it was Dash, who was formally dressed, standing at attention as he waited to assist her into the vehicle. There were other carriages waiting behind it, to carry other servants and Giabella's trunks.

But she could only look at Dash and know that they would be alone together for hours.

"Good morning, Your Majesty," he said softly as he extended a gloved hand to assist her into the carriage. She took it, electricity flowing between them despite the leather that encased both their hands.

"Thank you, Dashiell," she said, ducking into the carriage. He said something to the driver, and then he swung in and took his place across from her. There were papers stacked next to him, items to go over as they traveled. It looked like any other time they'd done this.

It didn't feel like it.

As the time passed, what it *felt* was awkward. And she hated that. She had always been comfortable with Dash. It was the saving grace of her life at times during the last ten years.

After an hour had gone by and the silence felt as sharp as a blade, she cleared her throat.

"Have you..." She trailed off as he lifted his blue eyes to hers. God, what did she want to say? Meaningless small talk that filled the air, but did nothing else? She cleared her throat. "Would you..." She huffed out a breath of frustration at her lack of ability to find something to say to her dearest friend, her closest confidante.

He leaned forward and took her hands gently. "Yes?"

She stared at their entwined fingers and found her breath. "Do you ever think about the future?"

His expression changed slightly and he drew his hand from hers. "Always. It is my job to forever be thinking ten steps ahead."

She shook her head. "No—no, I don't mean about your profession, Dash. I mean...do you ever think of *your* future? Of our..." She turned her face.

His breath came shorter and she felt his gaze slide over her even if she didn't look at him. "*Your* future is whatever you wish it to be, Gia," he said softly.

Now she did look at him. "I suppose that is true."

His brow wrinkled. "You sound as though that troubles you?"

"I suppose it...it does," she admitted, and let out a sigh. "Everything is changing. I was raised to be a queen. The queen of this nation. The marriage to Alistair was arranged when I was a child and the wedding itself took place when I was hardly more than that. It wasn't a life I chose, but it has always been what I knew. And now..." She shook her head. "I sound so ungrateful, I know. I have been nothing but proud of how Ophelia has comported herself as queen these last few months. She's taken on all the duties with ease. And I support Grantham completely as he steers this country in a new and very exciting direction."

"I know that," Dash said. "And you don't sound ungrateful by any means. The world becoming wide open can be troubling. Frightening."

She nodded. "Yes. That is it. It's all a little frightening."

"Have you spoken to the children about it?"

Ducking her head, she whispered, "No."

"Why?"

"Protecting them, I suppose. I don't want to make any of them veer off their paths in order to take care of me."

"You think you have to do this alone," he said. A statement, not a question, from someone who knew her so well. She lifted her gaze back to his and was lost in a sea of blue. His pupils dilated as she did so and he cleared his throat. "You will never be alone, Gia."

Her lips parted at the roughness of his voice as he said that. At the pointed desire that she easily recognized in his stare. It seemed she was not the only one who was coming to the end of her rope when it came to the tension that had always hung between them.

A tension she wanted so desperately to relieve in the most pleasurable of ways, consequences be damned.

The carriage began to slow on their first scheduled stop for the day, and Dash blinked as if waking from a dream. "I'm sorry, Your Majesty," he breathed, turning his face as he stacked the items he'd been rifling through during their journey. "I'd forgotten this brief interlude to trade horses and stretch our legs. You will likely meet with the innkeeper and his wife, Horace and Rebecca Monroe."

He rattled off more facts, but he never looked at her. She frowned at how far he was pushing her away.

"Dash," she whispered after he'd talked for what felt like forever.

He cut himself off and glanced at her. "After this stop, I think it would be prudent for me to ride outside the carriage a while," he said. The door opened and he motioned her to exit. "Your Majesty."

Tears stung her eyes, but she blinked them away as she took the footman's hand and exited the vehicle. She managed to greet the innkeeper and his wife by name, cooing over their lovely little inn and indulging in a tour. But all the while, her mind raced and she kept looking back at Dash over her shoulder.

He would always push her away, it seemed. No matter how much he wanted to be close, no matter how much she wanted it. He had on that terrible night when Alistair died and they'd nearly kissed. He'd done so any other time they got too near.

She had spent years with the power to snap her fingers and get what she wanted. But not him. And she feared the chances she had for such a thing were running out if she did not make a move he couldn't counter, couldn't deny and couldn't run from.

A few hours later Dash paced the terrace of Menington House restlessly, pausing occasionally to look out toward the sea. The rest of their journey had gone uneventfully. He had ridden outside the carriage, trying to maintain some sense of decorum and find his lost focus. Failing at both.

All he could think of was Gia's expression as they talked. The naked desire on her beautiful face. The need that mirrored his own.

Christ, it wasn't that he didn't know they both wanted this. But she'd always reined that in and he had followed suit. He'd reminded himself of the things that kept him from moving. At first her marriage, unhappy or not. Then the fact that she was queen and he a lowly servant. The fact that she had duties to fulfill and if he did not fulfill his own, then he risked her future.

He wanted in private and tried to tell himself that every side glance from her, every caught breath, every time she clung to his arm a little too tightly was a figment of his heated imagination. Remnants of erotic dreams that haunted him many a night.

That he was wrong in seeing those things in her even when they were right in front of his face, taunting him.

Today there had been no denying the heat between them, nor that it came from both sides of the equation. And it had taken every ounce of his control not to dig his fingers into her hair, pin her back against the carriage seat and kiss her like he'd wanted to kiss her for ten long years.

He blinked as the door from the house opened and she stepped outside. She had changed from her travel clothing to his favorite dress in her repertoire. Not a ballgown, though she always looked delicious in those. No, this was a gorgeous dark green-and-black striped silk dress with long sleeves and a scooped neck that just hinted at the lovely breasts beneath. It made her dark eyes even darker. The setting sun hit her hair and lit up the ruddy highlights one might not notice in candlelight.

He was struck mute for a moment as he looked at her, drank her in down to the detail, as if by memorizing her every curve and hollow that he would be fulfilled despite the distance he still had to keep.

"Good evening, Dashiell," she said.

Her soft voice broke the stupor she had put him in and he staggered toward her, hand outstretched toward her chair. "The staff thought that, with a night so lovely as this and with only the two of us in attendance, a terrace supper might be charming."

She smiled as she paced past the seat he had indicated, moving toward him in certain strides. He held his breath as she reached him, then stepped around him to the terrace. She braced both hands on the stone wall there and leaned forward, breathing in the sea air in a deep gulp.

"It is majestic," she whispered.

He continued looking at her, even though he knew she was talking about the huge rocky outcroppings just beyond the beach below the residence. "Always has been," he murmured.

Her cheeks filled with just a touch of color but she didn't address the comment, only turned back. "I'm happy to have a quiet meal tonight," she said, waiting as he pulled out her seat and then taking it. He took the one at her right. "Surely the few days will be very busy."

"We could go over the timeline again if you would like."

Usually she would answer in the affirmative. She always liked to review and re-review. He'd discovered that over his years in her service. Preparation was key for Giabella. She talked through things until she had every nuance in her mind.

Tonight, though, she shook her head. "You left your calendars in the carriage with me earlier today. I looked at them extensively during the journey."

He flinched ever so slightly at her gentle reminder that he'd abandoned her because of his lack of control. He didn't have a chance to apologize, though, because the supper began to be served.

Once their first course had been left before them, Giabella leaned closer. "Why don't we talk about happy things, Dash?"

She was giving him permission to find a path away from tension. He took it. During supper they talked about her children, especially Sasha, the daughter she had adopted more than fifteen years earlier. The child that had brought Dash to her when he presented the girl to the king and queen after she'd been orphaned.

The moment that had changed his life in so many ways. He saw Sasha as his own child, as much as Giabella's. A person they loved as deeply as they might have if they had created her together. That connection was a bond they'd built that had led to all the others.

"She is so very happy," Giabella sighed at last. "She and Thomas are very well matched."

He nodded. "Her last letter was gushing with joy. She looks forward to returning to Athawick shortly, though."

"Do you think she will have news soon for us?" Giabella asked, her gaze dancing.

He arched a brow. "Of a child, you mean?"

"Our first grandchild," Gia said, then her expression fell. "Because she sees you as her father. Far more than Alistair ever was." Her lips thinned.

He smiled as he thought of Sasha over the years. "If I am the father of her heart, then I am very proud to be so. And perhaps they *will* have news for us. Though I think any of your recently married children could be the first. They seem to be in a race to see who is most passionately in love."

Giabella blushed slightly. "That is certainly true. Any or all of them could tell me good news any day. I will like being a grand-mother, I think. A fine replacement title by the time it comes true, no matter what the outcome of this election. I will throw myself wholeheartedly into the endeavor. You will be scheduling me for changing nappies and embroidering little hats. A bore for you."

Dash swallowed as he set his fork down on his empty plate. She was offering him an opening to tell her about the offer Grantham had lodged to him weeks before. The future he had been hesitant to share with her because it would end this chapter of their lives together.

Perhaps all the chapters of their lives. Or perhaps it could begin another. He had no idea.

"Your Majesty," he began.

Something in her expression shifted. She set her napkin on the table and got to her feet, forcing him to do the same. She went back to the terrace wall. Once there, she pivoted. "I would like to walk on the beach."

He blinked. "It is...dark, Your Majesty."

"The moon is beginning to rise," she protested. "And I'm sure there is a lantern we can carry. Please, Dash, I will not have another chance this trip, with us leaving so early in the morning."

He should refuse her. But how could he? She was his sovereign, for one. And more than that, he did not ever wish to disappoint her.

He smiled and shook his head. "Or course. Let me make the arrangements."

She inclined her head and he entered the house, finally able to draw a full breath when he wasn't directly next to her. He could do this. Be alone with her. He'd been doing it for so many years, he could remember how.

He had to.

CHAPTER 4

Giabella's hands were shaking as she and Dash walked down the path toward the beach together, the lantern in his hand swinging between them. They were as alone as they ever got. Two guards would follow at a distance where they could be called if needed, but they would never interfere.

And that meant she had every opportunity to speak frankly to the man at her side. Not that she had done so at supper. She'd meant to. But she'd looked into his eyes and feared…feared what he would do if she said the truth. If she asked for what she wanted from a man who had always anticipated any need she had.

But this one was far more complicated.

Remi had said something to her before she left, and with every step it echoed in her ears. That she deserved to be happy. That she deserved what her children had found. Passion. Love. A future.

Would she regret it if she didn't at least attempt for one of those things with the man at her side? She already knew the answer.

They reached the sand and she stopped. "May I?" she asked, holding out a hand.

He moved toward her and she gently rested her fingers against his shoulder. She heard the catch of his breath as she balanced on his sturdy frame and removed first one slipper, then the other. She had already removed the stockings while he got the lantern, and her bare toes sank into the sand as she laughed.

"I love the way it feels," she said, and released him reluctantly to walk off toward the sea. The tide was higher at night, and as the wave swept in she lifted her skirt a fraction and let the cold water swirl around her feet.

He set the lantern down at the place where the sand met the sea grass behind her so when he moved to her side, all that lit them was the moonlight.

She didn't dare look at him as she said, "Earlier tonight you said something to me and I have been pondering it ever since."

"And what is that?" he asked, not dodging the waves that lapped around his boots.

She drew a long breath and continued to stare up at the moon and out toward the horizon in the dark. "You said that I wouldn't be alone as I navigate this new path I'll walk."

"You won't be. You have so many people who are at your side."

Now she did dare to turn toward him. His face was in half-shadow, half-light, and his gaze glittered. She shook her head. "That isn't why. Dash, I have never been alone since the moment you came into my life all those years ago. You've always been there. As my secretary, but also as my friend. And as a man I…I…"

She trailed off and couldn't continue. She didn't know how to exactly. What she felt for Dash was so complicated. It had been stifled for so long that labeling it felt dangerous and wrong.

So instead she moved toward him. For once, he didn't step back, and her chest nearly brushed his. They stared at each other for what felt like an eternity, though it was really only the span of a few shallow breaths. She lifted her hand, her fingers trembling as she touched him.

She had never touched his face. His beard was soft against her fingertips, his cheek tightening as he clenched his jaw. She glided her hand up, cupped it around the back of his neck as she leaned in.

She wanted to take his mouth but didn't dare, so instead she pressed her lips against the same cheek she had stroked a second before.

He stayed frozen for a beat, but then he slowly, deliberately, turned his face into hers. Their lips brushed gently and then…well, then the world exploded.

He wrapped his arms around her with a deep, guttural groan and tugged her flat against his chest. She fisted one hand into the thick hair at the base of his skull and wrapped the other around his shoulder, lifting into him as their lips parted and the kiss deepened into something wild and passionate.

All the longing of fifteen years, all the desire she had never been able to express, all the emptiness and loneliness, all the erotic dreams she had to deny…it all poured out of her. Into him. And he poured the same back.

She had never felt anything like it, this burning desire that seemed to grow and grow rather than diminish as their tongues tangled helplessly. The heat of it spread through her entire body, settling in her trembling fingertips, her tightening nipples, her throbbing sex. And she wanted him even more, which she had never believed was possible.

His hands gripped at her, like he could somehow bring her even closer, and he kept making the softest sounds of pleasure deep in his chest. This was escalating. Soon it would be out of control and she wanted nothing more than for him to break at last and lower her back on the sand to have his wicked, wild way with her.

It was like she sent that thought to him because he stopped kissing her. He drew back, staring down at her in the moonlight and then a look of utter horror crossed his handsome face. Slowly, he released her, steadying her before he backed away a long step.

She felt cold, empty, in the wake of losing his touch. She stared at him, willing herself to say something that would fix the expression on his face, but she couldn't. She, a woman raised to always know exactly what to say, and this time there was nothing. Nothing but desire that she had no words for. Regret that she dared not speak. Hope that she couldn't feel because hope was always shattered in the end.

So she only said his name. "Dash."

He shook his head and backed away another long step. "I-I'm sorry," he whispered.

Then he pivoted away, leaving her with only a lantern on the sand and a throbbing body she feared would never be fulfilled or satisfied again.

Dash couldn't see as he raced up the bluff away from Gia. It wasn't because of the darkness of the night, it was because his vision was blurred with desire and remorse. He staggered onto the grass at the top of the bluff and found the two guards, who had trailed them to a space near the beach, waiting there. They straightened as he reached them.

"H-her Majesty will need assistance when she is ready to return to the residence," he managed to mumble.

One of the guards nodded and headed toward the shore where Dash had left Gia. He continued to race his way to the house like the fires of hell itself were on his back. But no, not hell. Passion. The fires of a passion he never should have unleashed.

Because now he knew what the Queen of Athawick tasted like. And nothing could ever be the same.

He somehow managed to make it back to the house, up the back stair to his chamber there. A servant's chamber, and it was a stark reminder of their entirely disparate positions. She was queen of a nation. He was the man who kept her schedule. There was a wall there, one that existed for a thousand very good reasons. And he had crossed it. Allowed her to cross it, he supposed, because she had been the one who touched him first.

God, the way her hands felt as they brushed across his face. The way her expression softened with desire, the way her lower lip trembled. And then…then the way she tasted: sherry from supper, mint…her. She tasted like *her* and he wanted to memorize every different hint of that, from her lips to her skin to places he shouldn't even think about.

But he couldn't stop now. Fantasies he had always kept at bay save for passionate dreams bombarded him now. Forcing him to imagine what it would have been like to finally take what he'd always wanted. To have her the way he so longed to have her. To show her his heart, give it to her fully, by pleasing her body.

His cock throbbed, and he cursed as he flopped back on the bed and stared at the ceiling above him. He had to stop this. It was a mistake and she would realize that soon enough. He couldn't moon over it, moon over her. He couldn't look at her and think about what sound she would make when she came against his fingers or his tongue or his cock.

"Jesus," he grunted, and swiftly unfastened the fall front of his trousers. There was only one way to ease this, it seemed. Indulging it just this once, then never ever again.

He caught his hard cock in hand, stroking over the flesh once, twice. He allowed his eyes to flutter shut and his imagination ran wild. To images of tonight, when he'd finally let his lips touch Giabella's. To the sound she'd made as she lifted into him with desperation and pure desire.

And then he went further. Imagining how easy it would have been to back her into the soft sea grass. To lower her into the softness. To hitch up her skirt and slide his fingers along her inner thigh, past the slit in her drawers, into the dewy heat of her sex.

He spit on his hand and continued to stroke, lifting into the pleasure as he imagined gently fingering her, watching her face as she writhed beneath him, feeling her pulse around him as she came and then burying himself in her while she was still fluttering with release. Taking her, plunging into her over and over while he kissed her and she moaned into his mouth.

Pleasure ripped through him at that image and he pumped

harder, twisting against the bed before he came in an eruption of long-denied pleasure that seemed to last forever and echo through every nerve ending in his body.

When it was over, he opened his eyes, digging for a handkerchief to clean himself up. He shook his head. Now this was done. He could control himself again.

He had to. Because what had happened on the beach wasn't something that could happen again. He'd resigned himself to that fact a very long time ago and he couldn't trick himself into thinking there was any other future for him now.

CHAPTER 5

As the sound of cheering crowds grew louder around her, Giabella pulled back the curtain on the carriage and waved to her people gathered outside. Her arrival in Southern Athawick was to fanfare, some natural and some she had to assume was created by staff. That was the way of these sorts of public events.

The gate to the official residence where she was staying opened and the crowd surged, waving and shouting her name in the most supportive way.

She settled back and stared across at the empty seat opposite her. Dash had, yet again, not ridden with her during the journey this day. In fact, she had hardly seen him since their passionate kiss the night before.

The one that had been haunting her ever since. Perhaps it didn't do the same for him. Oh, she'd felt the power of his kiss. She wasn't going to pretend she hadn't. But that didn't mean that he liked how he felt. It didn't mean he wanted to want her.

And perhaps he just had more control over himself than she did.

The carriage stopped and the door opened a moment later. She caught her breath as Dash, himself, leaned in, offering his hand as he had done an infinite number of times. She took it, trying not to suck in her breath when they touched, and came out onto the drive.

"The counts are here," he said softly, taking up the position he'd always held.

She nodded once and they fell into their usual roles. He gently reminded her of facts about those they met when she needed them, allowing her to greet those around her in a far more personal way than she might have done on her own. She felt the warmth of him just at her side with every step. The weight of what was between them.

At last she reached the final person in the line of those aristocrats here to greet her. Count Hadley, who presided over the eastern part of the island. She normally had no strong feelings one way or another about these sorts of men. She had seen them come and go many times over the years and the royal family involved themselves as little as possible in judgment when it came to those in power.

But Hadley was the exception. Giabella glanced up and down the man's lean, tall frame and she despised him. After all, he had linked himself to Grantham's former courtier, Blairford. A man who had manipulated the unrest in the country, physically threatened several members of the family and had shot Dash in the arm not so long ago.

Her heart throbbed at the thought and it took all her many years of training to keep a restrained expression. "Count Hadley, how lovely to see you," she said, and knew her tone was icy cold.

Hadley seemed not to notice. He inclined his head slightly...very slightly. "Your Majesty. At least for a while longer, eh?"

"Quite," she said.

"I hope I'll have a chance to speak to you," he said. "I have some thoughts and concerns about—"

She held up a hand. "At the reception, Hadley, please."

"But—" Hadley protested.

She moved on and Dash stepped between them. "I shall ensure

you have a moment to speak to the queen when it is more convenient to her," he said, but she heard the strain in his voice as much as it had been in hers.

Hadley harrumphed but made no further effort to speak to her. She moved to the top of the stairs leading into the house and stopped there. "I look forward to connecting with you all at length at the reception in an hour's time. Until then, make yourselves comfortable."

There were bows and murmurs of approval, but Giabella hardly heard them as she entered the house. She handed over her gloves to the waiting butler. "Ah, Livingston, so wonderful to see you again."

"And you, Your Majesty," the older servant said. "The staff is eager to make your stay as pleasant as possible."

She nodded and smiled warmly at the man before she made her way toward the stairs. Dash was at her side immediately.

"I despise that Hadley must be included after what he did," she said under her breath.

"I understand," Dash said softly. "I feel the same way. But there was no evidence linking the man to Blairford's actual plans for a coup. He would have been...at least in theory...a pawn, not someone who was aware."

"I can well believe that," she muttered as they reached the top of the stairs and moved toward her chamber at the end of the hall. "The man has always been a pompous fool."

She opened the door and began to step in, but was surprised when Dash stayed put. She wrinkled her brow. "You aren't...you aren't coming in to discuss the night further before I ready myself?"

He cleared his throat and his gaze moved from hers. "I think it might be wise, Your Majesty, if I did not."

She swallowed. He would not look at her and she ached at the loss of him even in that small way. "Dash," she began.

He reached into the inside pocket of his jacket and retrieved a small stack of papers. She could see they were written on in his smooth, even handwriting that she knew better than her own. "I have prepared a full briefing for you to review as you prepare for the evening."

"I see," she said, trying desperately to meter her tone the same way he did. "And will you abandon me tonight, then?"

Now he did dart his gaze to hers. "Not abandoning, Gia—Your Majesty," he said swiftly. "I will be at your side as always once we reach the reception. I am just creating a distance I-I never should have closed. It is there for a reason, after all."

She pursed her lips, hating how hurt and disappointment washed over her. She stepped back. "I suppose it is," she said softly. "Then I will see you tonight."

She turned away and flinched when the door shut behind her. She pushed the pain from her face as Betsy walked in from the other room. The maid's expression was bright as she brought out the two gowns they had packed for this event. Giabella sighed and put away her thoughts as a woman on this subject. Tonight she was queen and she would need to act as such.

At the very least, it would make the sting of what felt like rejection fade a little. At least she hoped it would.

From the moment he'd first met her, Dash had always been impressed by Giabella. She wore her role as queen with an ease that many might try to replicate, but none could.

Tonight, as the reception in her honor wore on, he watched her move from aristocrat to aristocrat, engaged with each one like he was the most interesting person in the room. She laughed even when the jokes weren't funny, she leaned in when someone told her something personal or painful, she gave both a sense of regal distance but also warm humanity to her role and to the monarchy in itself.

If she were still upset about what had transpired between them on the beach the night before, she didn't show it to those in the room as she moved from person to person, connecting with them all. She didn't even show it to Dash. When they'd met in the hallway outside, she had smiled and nodded to him, as usual. The only indication that anything had changed between them was that her smile didn't reach her dark eyes.

And that she had called him Mr. Talbot before they entered the room. Oh, how that moment had stung. Even though he was the one who insisted that distance between them was important.

He shook away the thoughts and looked at her through the crowd again. She had been standing with Count Friskar for a while now. Under normal circumstances she might send Dash the very specific look that told him she needed to be rescued from a conversation that had gone on too long. But the family liked the count and she seemed not to be in need of interruption on his part. Still, Dash moved a step closer in case that changed.

Giabella laughed and his heart stuttered. By God, she was the most beautiful woman he'd ever met in his entire life. And when she was happy…he was happy.

But the moment passed quickly enough. Another of the counts approached, Hadley, and her smile fell back into the false one she wore for people she didn't know or like. He touched his forearm out of habit. Dash could feel the faint throb of the raised scar where he'd been shot saving Grantham's life half a year ago.

They spoke for a moment and Friskar bowed as he excused himself. Hadley was talking swiftly, Giabella arched a brow. She said something and Hadley nodded, motioning her toward the terrace beyond the receiving room windows. Dash caught his breath and followed them at a respectful distance out onto the terrace that had grown dark during the evening's festivities.

Hadley was leading Giabella toward the terrace wall and Dash stepped into the shadow to watch their interaction, his body coiled to come to the rescue, his gaze focused on Gia's face so he would see the moment when she required interruption. Because this was what he'd been for a decade and a half…he would not change it. Not until he had to. Not until the very end.

~

Giabella kept a serene expression on her face, but her stomach turned as she took in her companion. She had never liked Count Hadley, nor his father before him. Pompous men too full of their power, counting what they felt they were owed rather than taking seriously their duty to their people. And Hadley the younger, the one who was chattering on slightly drunkenly at her side, had always stared at her and her daughters in a certain way. Leering when he thought no one noticed.

Disgusting creature.

"But I asked you to accompany me onto the terrace so we might have a private conversation as the evening winds down," Hadley said, and Giabella forced herself to attend.

"You know you can make an appointment with my secretary," she said softly, "if you wish for a discussion. Or come to the capital and meet with Grantham."

There was the slightest twitch to Hadley's cheek at the mention of her son. Once again she thought of this bastard's involvement with a man who had plans to kill for power. Was Hadley more involved in that than anyone knew? Or was he just as he appeared: a mindless rube who blindly reached for anything he could get?

"But why not take advantage of these more pleasant circumstances?" Hadley asked, and Giabella supposed he meant his tone to be smooth rather than desperate.

"I suppose," she said. "Though I do have farewells to say as the evening winds down, so perhaps we should have this conversation you'd like."

Hadley cleared his throat. "Of course. Your Majesty, I come to you as a man desperate to protect his country. And you may be the only one with influence enough to aid me."

She arched a brow. As if the Hadleys had ever given a damn about their country. "I'm afraid I'm not sure what you mean."

"Let me clarify. You have been part of a royal family all your life, first in Everlay and then here in Athawick. You cannot truly wish to see that long tradition dissolved by this foolish notion of your son."

She pressed her lips together hard. "I have spent a lifetime in service to this country. Service, my lord: *that* is the imperative word to focus on. In their best, the aristocracy serves the people. And in this moment, the people are saying it isn't what they want. I bow to their desires and full-throatedly support Grantham's brave decision to change the course of our island."

Hadley opened and shut his mouth. "But the upheaval, the loss, the…the power…"

"Are you speaking in terms of the country, or your own loss, sir?" she asked softly.

His expression hardened a fraction, but he didn't respond. She doubted he was able, for she had likely hit upon the truth. "I realize that change is always difficult, my lord. But some pains make for the future, and so we must endure them in the knowledge that better things are on the horizon…for everyone, not just for a ruling few." She inclined her head slightly. "And now I should return to the others. Our time together is coming to a close for now, and as I said, I would like to say my goodbyes."

She pivoted to walk away, but Hadley shocked her by catching her wrist. He pulled her back, none too gently, and she saw the wild desperation increasing in his gaze, as well as smelled the hint of whisky on his breath. "Now wait just a moment," he growled.

She tugged at her arm. "You would do well to recall who I am, Lord Hadley," she said, glad her voice sounded firmer than her shaking fingers were at present. "I am queen mother of this nation."

"Not for much longer," he all but spat. "*That* is the future you are discussing with such fervor, you know. What will you do when you have no power, no protection?"

She opened her mouth to retort, but before she could, Dash

seemed to appear out of nowhere. He stepped up to Hadley, wedging himself between them and forcing the count to release her wrist at last. Dash pressed his hands to the other man's chest and pushed hard.

"Back up," he said, his tone darker and more dangerous than anything she'd heard from him in all their years together.

"How dare you?" Hadley huffed as he regained his balance against the wall edge.

"I'm calling the guards," Dash said, shooting her a look.

Giabella caught his arm before he could wave for attention from the guards stationed inside. "Wait," she said, and lowered her voice. "He was drunk, and creating a scene with him might only make things worse."

Dash met her gaze and pursed his lips. "Very well, Your Majesty."

Hadley smirked. "You're just a servant—don't forget it."

"And *you* are just a fool," Dash said, leaning closer. "And if you ever put your hands on her again, I will make sure that you regret it."

Giabella wrapped her fingers tighter around Dash's forearm, attempting to draw him back away from Hadley. The count might be losing power, but he could still wield it over Dash if he chose.

"Dash," she said softly.

He looked back at her and their eyes met. He nodded slightly and stepped away, catching her hand to tuck it into the crook of his elbow as he moved her away from the man who had been so bold as to touch her, to *grab* her.

They had made it two steps away when Hadley called out, "I can see why you might be so interested in those with no rank, Your Majesty. Now it makes more sense."

Dash released her and crossed back to the man in three long steps. Giabella lunged toward him, but it was too late. Dash punched the man, rocking him back on his arse against the low wall where he then towered over him, blue eyes wild in the moonlight.

"Disparage the queen again and you *will* be sorry," Dash said, and then moved back to her.

He escorted Giabella back inside where the crowd was already thinning. She bent her head, cheeks flaming and hands shaking from the entirely unpleasant encounter.

"I must say my goodbyes," she murmured as Dash moved her toward the door to the reception hall.

Dash shook his head. "They will see you soon enough for the next event," he insisted.

She didn't argue. After all, he had been doing what was best for her for years. And she had begun to shake so hard, she feared she wouldn't be able to do her duty even if she insisted upon staying and trying.

He maneuvered her down the hallway and up the stairs, down the hall to her chamber, where he guided her inside. It was only when he released her to shut the door that the full impact of what had just happened hit her. She covered her face with her hands and let out a long, shaky sigh.

She felt him move even without looking at him, and his arms folded around her, drawing her against his chest, enveloping her in his warmth. She softened against him, reveling in the feel of him against her.

"I'm sorry," he murmured against her ear. "I should have come over sooner. I never should have let him speak to you alone in the first place considering his history. That he frightened you is unforgiveable."

She lifted her head and met his gaze. "Frightened me? What frightens me is that you could have created trouble for yourself by defending me so strenuously. I thought entirely of you, Dash."

He blinked down at her and then his gaze shifted. His pupils dilated, his hands tightened around her, and slowly…God, so slowly, his mouth lowered. He was going to kiss her again.

And when he did, it was going to shift the world once more.

CHAPTER 6

When Dash claimed her lips with his, Giabella couldn't find control. Just like the night before on the beach, it was like someone set off a bomb in her body and all she could do was lift helplessly into him as she opened her lips and welcomed him inside.

Only this time they weren't in public, with guards a few steps away. They were in her bedroom, and if she locked her door, no one would interrupt. Whatever happened would be private.

It gave her boldness, and she deepened the kiss, tasting him, leaning into him, letting him feel how she wanted him without barrier or hesitation. And his hungry response told her he was in no more control than she. His fingers clawed at her back, his tongue drove hard past her lips, he kept making greedy sounds of pleasure and drive and need that made her entire body tremble in a way she'd almost forgotten.

She didn't want it to end. She needed it not to end.

She pulled away and stared up at him. Their panting breaths were matched, but she still saw questions in his eyes. Hesitations she needed to erase if she wanted this, wanted him.

She moved toward the door. Once there she turned her back to it, leaned against it, watching him as she reached behind her to slowly turn the key in the lock.

His eyes went wide. "Gia," he whispered.

She shivered at the sound of her name from his lips. He was the only person in this world who had ever called her that shortened version of her name. Like a secret language that bound them together.

A thread she wanted to use to tug him closer.

"Don't deny me," she whispered. "Tell yourself it's only for tonight, Dash. Forget everything else. Just let me have tonight."

She expected arguments, reasoning, a battle for what they both wanted. There were none. Instead, he crossed to her in three long steps and then pushed her back harder against the door. His mouth covered hers, his hands dug into her hair, sending pins clattering away onto the floor around them.

She gasped against his lips, shocked by how he set her on fire. He made her tremble. He made her feel only like a woman, not a queen or a dignitary or an office that a dozen women had held before her.

He made her feel beautiful and alive, and she never wanted it to end.

His mouth moved from her lips, down the side of her throat. He sucked there, hard…harder…until her fingers dug into his forearms and she let out a mewling sound of desire. She found the buttons along the front of his jacket and tugged them free, shoving her hands into the warmth trapped there, letting her fingers feel him through his waistcoat and linen shirt beneath. His stomach flexed when she flattened her palm against it, and he grunted her name again, this time muffled by her flesh. She felt the two syllables vibrate against her throat and she arched against him helplessly in response.

The jacket crumpled behind him as she shoved it away and she managed to wind her fingers into his cravat, desperate to untangle the knots as he brushed his lips to the hollow of her throat and down to the soft patch of skin beneath it. He brought fire in his wake, making her nerves go crazy with sensation as he sucked and licked and kissed.

She felt his hands on the buttons along her spine. His fingers moved swiftly, surely...but of course they did. This was Dash—the man was a model of efficiency. He would, of course, be the same even in seduction. There was comfort in that. Ease and understanding that she clung to as she finally managed to unknot the cravat and began to unwrap it.

His mouth found hers again and her hands faltered at the slide of his tongue against hers. Slower now, easier like he was trying to make this moment they were stealing last.

Oh, how she wanted that, too. Wanted it so desperately. She found herself leaning into him, hands clutching at the ends of his neck wrap helplessly. She was shocked when she felt his hands against her back, only her chemise separating them. He had done wonders while he distracted her with his mouth.

He drew back, blue eyes glinting in the firelight, and tracked every moment as he slowly glided her gown forward, down over her arms, left it to dangle at her waist. It had been years since a man saw her like this. Her late husband was the last. He had not looked so... astounded as Dash did. Dash looked at her like she was the most beautiful creature in the world. Like he was stunned to have found her, to be near her.

She could almost believe it. Preen about it. Own it with the same certainty that she owned her everyday duties to the country.

"Gia," he murmured, holding out a hand. He traced the bare flesh of her arm with his fingertips. He cupped her elbow and drew her closer. "My God."

She swallowed hard, keeping her gaze locked with his as she slid her fingers beneath the chemise straps. With a deep breath, she folded the undergarment down over her arms, pushed it to join the dress. She was naked from the waist up.

She was not as young as she'd once been. Who was, after all? She knew she wasn't as firm as she'd been at twenty. She wasn't as smooth. But she watched Dash watch her and she felt utterly, exquisitely beautiful through his eyes.

And utterly and forever hot with desire for him. She caught his hand, which he had dropped to his side when she pushed her clothing away and lifted it. Gently she placed it against her breast, sucking in a breath at the weight of him. At the rough slide against sensitive flesh.

If he had seemed stunned into stone a moment before, forcing his touch woke him. He caught her arm and tugged her closer, even as his opposite hand began to stroke her breast. He swirled a thumb around her nipple, making her remember how responsive that part of her could be. She arched against him, gasping out his name in the quiet just before he lowered his head and licked her.

She dug her hands into his hair, holding him closer as he sucked her nipple, then swirled his tongue around it over and over. She found herself lifting her hips in time, seeking release, seeking more, seeking that ultimate joining that she had told herself would never, could never happen.

Now she needed it more than breath. She would have traded anything to have it and have him. The alternative seemed, in this charged moment, to be a fate worse than death.

He backed her through the antechamber and into the bedroom behind it. Her fire was lit and it cast dancing light across her bed. They moved toward it, one body, never breaking their kiss. His hands roved over her, down her bare back, tangling in the gown around her waist, shoving it aside the moment he had reached the bed.

She wanted to cover herself. For a brief, but powerful moment, she recognized she was basically naked with him. Emotionally as well as physically. But as his hands trailed down and he cupped her bare backside, pulling her tighter against him, the flare of fear and embarrassment was erased.

All that was left was the wet pulse of need, throbbing between her legs in the same rhythm with which he kissed her. She never broke that kiss as she unbuttoned his shirt with shaking hands. At some point he pulled away just long enough to remove it and then ducked his head to kiss her again.

"I want to look at you," she gasped as she flattened her hand against his chest.

He made a rumbling sound deep within that same chest, but he didn't deny her. Not that he ever had in all the time they'd been together. He stepped back and let her look.

He was wonderful. Just as wonderful as she had pictured in her heated dreams over the years. Just as she'd fantasized as she touched herself until she came undone while her husband slept with his mistresses in the next room.

Dash was everything. Lean muscle tapered to trim hips with a peppering of hair that trailed into his trouser waist. He moved to embrace her again and she caught her breath at the scar on his left forearm.

He followed her gaze to it and held it out. "It's not so bad, Gia."

"You nearly died. For Grantham." She lifted her gaze. "For me. Always for me."

He nodded slowly. "Everything for you, Gia. For right or for wrong, for good or for bad."

She traced the scar with her forefinger and then dragged it up his arm, across his shoulder, down the middle of his body until she hooked it into the waist of his trousers.

"Show me," she whispered, and tugged him closer.

He kissed her once more. Their fingers tangled together as they both worked to undo the fall front of his trousers. It fell away and she looked down at his cock.

She shivered at the look of him, hard and ready for her. And when she touched him, taking him in hand to stroke him, he shivered for her, as well.

"Please," she whispered, whimpered, and he nodded.

He lowered her back on the bed and she shifted to rest on the pillows. He joined her, putting himself between her spread legs.

He reached between them, and for the first time he touched her there.

The stroke of his fingers against her sensitive flesh was enough to make her arch in pleasure. He parted her outer lips and she knew he found her wet for him, ready for him. After all, she'd been waiting so long. This moment was a culmination of over a decade of foreplay when she really thought about it.

He found her clitoris and circled there, gently at first, then harder and faster. She turned her face into her shoulder, biting her lip to keep the gasps and moans from filling the room. He was expert at this, just as he had been at every other thing she needed for so long.

She was right on the edge of release now, the pulse of pleasure mounting with every flick of his fingers. He caught her lips with his, driving deep with his tongue, and the orgasm hit with an intensity that surprised her. She gripped one hand against his back while she fisted the other in the coverlet beneath her. She jerked against his hand, moaning his name into his mouth as the waves washed over her again and again and again.

She had hardly begun to come down when he stroked the head of himself against her entrance. She widened her legs farther and broke their kiss. Together they watched as he pushed inside of her, stretching her and filling her in a way she'd almost forgotten felt so good.

"Don't stop," she begged, gripping his forearms. "Please don't stop."

"I would never," he promised, and then he thrust. Gently, at first, giving her time to remember this glorious feeling of being full and how much pleasure each slide of a man inside of her brought.

No, not any man. This man. Because it had never been like this before and she doubted any other man could ever make it like this again. She dug her fingers into his hair with one hand and clung to his back with the other as she rose to meet his thrusts. They ground together gently, slowly, deeply, and then faster and with a hunger that was almost frightening in its intensity.

The pleasure he had given with his fingers returned now, but it was deeper than before. Sharper when his pelvis rotated against hers. She gasped against his mouth and he nipped her lower lip gently, their breath mingling. She arched against him, pleasure overtaking a second time. She pulsed around him, digging her fingers into his flesh and loving the way he groaned low in his chest, as if her pleasure was his pleasure.

His thrusts increased as he drew her through the crisis, faster, more out of control. The veins in his neck were outlined as he tossed his head back and grunted her name. He withdrew and pulsed into his hand as he came. She drew him down, kissing him again, reveling in the feel of his heat around her. Reveling in this moment that had finally come and that she never wanted to end. Even though she knew there would be consequences to it.

Because there always were.

Dash felt like his nerves had all fired at once and were now overly sensitized. Every time Giabella stroked her fingers along his spine or pressed her mouth to his throat, he was wracked by another shiver of pleasure. Nothing had ever been like this before, not in all his years.

And yet as passion faded a fraction, the reality of what they'd done began to color the moments. He stared down at her, this woman in his arms and couldn't help but see her as what she was. A queen. His employer.

His emotions overwhelmed him, and he rolled away from her, staring up at the ceiling above. He had made love to Giabella. And it was perfect and wonderful. But it had been a mistake. One he'd been fighting to avoid for so very long.

"Please don't look that way," she said softly, moving to her side and propping herself up on her elbow to look down at him.

"Look what way?" he asked.

She cocked her head. "You know me so well after all these years—please grant that I know you too, Dash. I can see all the trouble on your face. All the regret and worry about what just happened. You are strategizing your way out of it and away from me."

"How can I not, Gia…Your Majesty?" he asked.

Now she sat up and her expression grew more pointed. "I think Gia or Giabella is more appropriate when you are talking to a woman you just bedded."

He huffed out a breath. "We can't pretend that you are only that, though, can we? You are too clever to disagree. I have done something…something I never should have done."

She flinched and her head bent. She drew a few long breaths. "This is what I wanted. This is what I…" She looked at him now, held his gaze. "This is what I've always wanted, Dash. From the first moment I met you, everything else be damned."

"Gia," he whispered, moved beyond measure at that confession that stabbed into the very heart of him. The heart that loved her so completely. That she had felt anything similar for him all this time was beautiful and utterly heartbreaking all at once.

"We have to be honest now, don't we?" she asked. "Or at least I must be. I wanted you and I still want you. And if this destroys all we've been to each other—"

"Queen and servant," he said.

She shook her head. "Always more than that. You are my most constant friend and confidante. My most constant everything. This cannot make me lose that. Please tell me it hasn't changed our future."

He shut his eyes. Her words hung in his mind, rang in his ears. *We have to be honest now.* He'd been avoiding that honesty for days, weeks. And now that this amazing moment had happened between them, he knew he couldn't do it anymore.

He sat up and cupped her face, sinking into the softness of her skin, the way her pupils dilated when he touched her. "I must tell you something," he said softly. "I should have said it a while ago."

Her lips parted and she straightened up. "What is it?"

"I...I've been offered a position by the king," he admitted slowly. "In his new government, should the election go as we assume it will in a few weeks' time. Not as a servant, but as an official advisor. A member of his...I don't know what he'll call it...circle of advisors? Cabinet?"

"Dash," she murmured.

"I should have told you sooner," he said. "But I didn't know how. But when you speak about the future, I need you to know that. And that I...I would like to take the position."

~

Giabella stared at Dash, stunned into silence. Her hands shook and her ears rang as she tried to process what he'd said. When he'd said he had to tell her something, she had foolishly thought, for one blinding moment, that it might be that he loved her. But it wasn't that. It was this news that he was leaving her.

It felt like rejection, even though she knew in her heart that it wasn't. It was a grand opportunity, one he had earned through good and faithful service, through having the best interest of their family and nation at heart.

But that didn't change the abject terror that gripped her at the thought that she would lose him. And she *would* lose him. He wouldn't serve as her secretary once he took an official government post. She couldn't interfere with that.

But she had been thinking more and more about her future lately. And she might not know much, but she knew it didn't include having such proximity to government. It set such a bad precedent, to tell the people that they were going to be free to choose, then load their government with the same family they had wished to be free from in the first place.

It felt like something Alistair would do.

"Giabella, please say something," Dash said, getting to his feet and grabbing for his trousers. Putting a barrier between them that she hated.

She swallowed hard. "I think you would be very good in that sort of role," she said. "And that you would be a fool not to take it."

"Even if it means things would change?" he asked.

She slowly got to her feet, trying not to be so self-conscious about her nudity. It was hard when his gaze flitted down her and his eyes filled with renewed desire. "Things have changed already," she said, taking his hand and lifting it to her heart. "We both know it."

He nodded and touched her cheek with his other hand, tracing the line of her cheekbone with his index finger. "Yes, they have."

"But I said it before and I'll say it again: I wanted this, Dash." She felt so vulnerable saying what she had to say next. "And if you are going to take a position, end our…our partnership soon…then this trip may be our only time to explore this thing that has bubbled between us for years."

His brow wrinkled. "Are you…what are you saying?"

"You know what I'm saying," she whispered. "I'm saying I want to do this again. Over and over again, with you. I want to pretend, for the next little while, that what we did is something that can be repeated. I want to be with you."

He stared at her a beat, two, and she felt tears begin to sting her eyes.

"Please tell me I'm not a fool, that you want the same thing."

She saw the fight on his face. How he was torn between duty and desire, torn between whatever he considered right versus what he plainly wanted. And she held her breath to see what side would win.

In the end, he flexed his hand against her skin, dragging it from her heart to cup her face. He leaned in and kissed her, slowly, deeply, gently as he backed her to the bed they had just vacated. "I want you, Gia," he murmured as they fell across the mattress, his hands moving over her skin, his mouth claiming hers with hunger and purpose.

She pushed out everything else, all her fears and questions and sank into what this was. The rest could wait. She intended to savor every stolen moment.

CHAPTER 7

"Good morning, Your Majesty," Betsy said as she pushed open the curtains and filled Giabella's chamber with bright sunlight.

Giabella lifted a hand to her eyes and shivered at the delicious ache in her body. She'd had hardly any sleep thanks to Dash, who had only left her bed an hour before, but it didn't matter. Who needed rest when she now had such wonderful memories?

"It's a beautiful morning," she said, yawning as she sat up and dragged the covers around herself.

If Betsy thought it odd that her gown was lying on the floor in a pile or that she was naked in her bed, she said nothing and just went about the business of tidying up before she handed over Giabella's robe. She wrapped it around herself as she got up and moved to the window to stare out at the view of the grounds and the sea in the distance.

"I've a bath drawn in the other room," Betsy said. "And then I believe we agreed on the blue muslin to start the day."

"Perfect," Giabella said as she followed the maid into the attached room and the bath awaiting her.

Her morning went by as usual. Nothing could have been seen as extraordinary in the bath or how she was dressed or styled. She even managed to keep up a conversation with Betsy, laughing and chatting as she usually did with her longtime servant. And yet nothing about the day felt average.

She had made love to Dash. Over and over again, actually. She had found pleasure the likes of which she had never experienced. It was everything she had ever imagined or dreamed.

How could any day be typical after that?

At last she was ready. Betsy tweaked one last lock into place and smiled. "Perfect, as always, Your Majesty."

Giabella smiled as she got up and looked at herself in the full-length mirror by the door on the way out of the room. She felt pretty and ready to see the man who inspired the high color in her cheeks and renewed brightness in her eyes.

"Thank you, Betsy!" she called over her shoulder as she left the chamber and made her way downstairs to the breakfast room. As she entered, she found Dash at the table, staring at the door even though the paper was drooping in his hands. He pushed to his feet to greet her.

Heat entered her cheeks as she let her gaze sweep over him. No one would know he hadn't slept most of the night. He was perfectly pulled together, as always, in a muted gray waistcoat, every hair on his head and whisker of his beard in exact place.

"Good morning," she said, taking a step toward him before she stopped herself. There were others in the room. The footman who was bringing Dash his morning tea stopped to incline his head in acknowledgment.

She could not forget herself. Even if being in the same room as Dash made her do just that.

"Good morning, Queen Giabella," he replied, his tone a little rougher than usual, a little more intimate. God, how she loved when he said her name. Or groaned it against her skin.

She never wanted it to stop.

She moved to the sideboard and made herself a plate. Her tea was waiting when she returned and the servant was just leaving the room as she took her place and Dash returned to his. Once they were alone, she dared to reach out a hand and cover his.

"Good morning," she said again, this time with far more meaning.

His fingers flexed beneath hers and he smiled ever so slightly. "You are so beautiful that it almost hurts to look at you." Then he shook his head and cleared his throat, returning to the trusted servant he had always been. "I would ask how you slept—"

"My time in bed was wonderful," she interrupted with a wink. He shifted as if he was nervous, and she smiled at him again. "Dash, we are still us."

He blinked and she saw the understanding come into his eyes. Us. They had always been an us, for so many years she could barely remember what it had been like before he came into her life. Far more meaningless, certainly.

When had she fallen in love with him? She wondered it as she stared at him and the feeling became so clear that it almost played like music in the air. She loved him, so deeply and powerfully that it was twisted into her own soul. She could not have separated herself from it if she tried.

Had it happened the first time she met him? Was it when he'd come to work in the office of the queen a handful of years after? Had it come on slowly, a little bit at a time as he brought her tea and asked her questions and filled the emptiness of her life with his sure and steady presence? Or was it a thunderbolt that she didn't remember in the midst of a storm?

He cleared his throat. "I shall try to remember what *us* is like," he said, and slid his hand from hers to grab for the paperwork on the other side of his plate. "I have your itinerary, Your Majesty."

She pushed away her thoughts, her realization that would surely change the course of the rest of her life, and focused on what he was saying. "Yes, it is the farmers this morning, is it not?"

"Yes," he said. "You have a good memory, as always. And afterward, a pass through the orphanage that was just established on the island. Finally you'll have tea with the village ladies society."

"They were the ones who petitioned for the funds for the orphans, yes?" Giabella asked. "And made certain it was built and staffed accordingly."

He nodded. "Yes. I've heard it's a wonderful facility."

She sipped her tea. "I think we both have a strong connection to such an issue. When I look at orphans, all I can think about is Sasha that day you brought her to me…to the king and I, after she was orphaned."

He straightened slightly and she saw the softness that always came into his eyes when he spoke of Sasha. Although she had been adopted by the royal family, it had never been Alistair who treated her as her father should…it had always been Dash. In some way, she was their child, Dash and Giabella's.

She shivered at the thought and forced a smile. "I cannot wait to see it and meet the children. Is that the entirety of the day?"

"Yes," he said. "We left some time open for flexibility if you wish to add an event. And if nothing comes up, you and I get to have a lovely supper…alone."

She shifted slightly in her chair. "I will make sure I add nothing, then."

He chuckled and they finished their breakfast together. Giabella forced herself to be light, chatting with him as if nothing had changed. And yet every word and glance felt different now. Charged by the power of what they'd shared, what she felt for him, and what she had to look forward to with him later that night when they were truly alone.

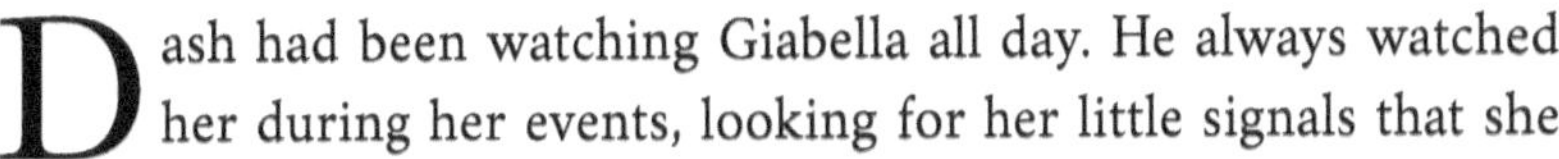

Dash had been watching Giabella all day. He always watched her during her events, looking for her little signals that she needed rescue, providing her with swift information so that everyone she met felt remembered and seen by her.

But today…today was different. Although they had made love and he felt closer to her than he'd ever allowed himself to be, he watched from more of a distance as she moved through the ladies' village society group, talking to each woman.

She was a marvel. She always was. There was no one better than her at soothing the ruffled feathers of pompous dignitaries or putting someone in power in their place with nothing more than a raised eyebrow.

But here…here she was truly in her element. She was easy with her people, her kindness and warmth genuine. All day people had lit up when they met her. If there had been unrest in this part of the island, the people seemed to be able to separate their desire for autonomy from their adoration of their queen. Everyone who spoke to her left with broad smiles and easier hearts. He could see her doing exactly what Grantham had wished: easing the tension.

That was Giabella's gift. And he had been fortunate enough to help her share it for over a decade. To watch her up close as she worked her magic on everyone in her life. And it was one of his greatest regrets that he wouldn't be at her side as she did the same in her future.

He would see her, of course. The palace would remain the official residence of the new leader of the country, at least for the first few years, and Giabella was so beloved that he had to believe she would be allowed to remain there the rest of her days.

But it wouldn't be the same.

Not that anything would be the same after this trip and what they'd done together.

She glanced toward him, and he jolted. There was her signal, the slight flutter of her lashes that told him she had talked too long to the same enthusiastic person and was ready to be kindly moved along.

He darted forward to her elbow and leaned in. Normally he

whispered gibberish, but today he murmured, "Ready to be alone again?"

She glanced up at him, her dark eyes snaring his with a message that was perfectly clear and powerfully erotic. Then she returned her attention to the ladies who had been attending her. "I'm afraid my secretary has reminded me of my next engagement. But I have enjoyed myself immensely and am so impressed by all of you and your dedication to the children of this nation."

The ladies all murmured and tittered with pleasure, and the leader of their society, Miss Bernard, stepped up. "Let me see you out, Your Majesty," she said.

Dash stepped away, trailing behind as the two women moved toward the foyer of the assembly hall and the royal carriage that awaited them there. He could hear Miss Bernard speaking to Giabella as they walked. "I want you to know, Your Majesty, that all of us are in complete support of King Grantham and his future as… what do they call it again?"

"Prime minister," Giabella supplied.

"Indeed. That all of us in the country, no matter race or creed or sex, are allowed to have a voice and a vote is…" Tears filled Miss Bernard's eyes. "Well, I know everyone is very excited to have a part in our island's next chapter. I hope you will pass those sentiments on to the king and his advisors."

Giabella turned toward her and caught both her hands. "I will, my dear. And I hope that I, as well as my son, will be welcome to call here again in the future. And that you will prepare reports on the orphanage and how we can further support your efforts."

"Thank you, Your Majesty," the woman said, curtsying low as Dash opened the carriage door for Giabella and took her hand to help her in.

"Good afternoon, Miss Bernard," he said with an incline of his head.

"Mr. Talbot," she returned.

He climbed into the carriage beside Giabella and settled in. The queen waved as they pulled away, smiling at the rapidly shrinking figure of Miss Bernard.

"I think that went well," she said.

He nodded. "Very well. But I never worry about that. You know exactly what you need to do every time."

She shook her head. "That is not true, but I appreciate the never wavering support you always provide."

Dash held her gaze for a moment, then reached forward and closed the curtain. Late afternoon light still crept in around the edges of the curtain, but the carriage was dim now.

She smiled slightly. "Ready for darkness, are you?"

He slowly eased to her side of the carriage and settled in next to her on the narrow bench. "I'm ready to do something I shouldn't with the entire village able to see."

She rested her hand on his chest and lifted into him as he lowered his mouth to hers. The kiss began as gentle, just the brush of his lips on hers. But now he knew how powerful they could be together and he couldn't ignore what he wanted. What she wanted as she fisted his lapels in her hands and let out a soft sigh of pleasure into his mouth.

He deepened the kiss, still going slowly, and sank into the flavor of her. The way her tongue brushed his own. The way the act of kissing her worked through his veins like a drug and woke all the nerves in his body.

"Dash," she murmured as she dragged her mouth from his and along his jawline.

"Hmmm?" He tried to find some way to focus, to come up for air.

She shivered as she rested her head against his shoulder. "I still can't believe we're doing this."

He wrapped his arms around her and kissed her temple lightly. "Because of our disparate positions?"

She glanced up at him. "No. It's just that this has been in the realm of dream for me for so long. Fantasy. I keep waiting to wake up every time you kiss me."

He smiled. "It's the same for me. I think neither of us could deny the tension has existed between us for a very long time."

"The first time I met you," she admitted softly, and her cheeks brightened. "My heart made this flutter it had never made before and I knew nothing could be the same."

He wrinkled his brow. "You'd never felt something like that before?"

"No." She laughed, but it was hollow. "Alistair was my arranged marriage. I was never allowed to even consider another man. I dutifully did as I was told. And I wanted to care for him, I truly did. But I never felt anything for him...except regret. And ultimately, contempt."

Dash nodded slowly. "I only knew you after years of your marriage to Alistair," he said carefully, not wanting to push where he could hurt her. "And I know your relationship was complicated."

She sighed. "It always was. He made it clear from the first day of our marriage that it would never be a love match. I was there to create his heirs and spares, as well as complete my duties as queen and faithful wife. All while he kept his mistresses, sometimes right under my nose."

Dash flinched. "I did not know that happened from the start."

"Yes. I grew to hate him at first. And then to feel...nothing at all. I'm not sure which was worse." She touched his face. "*You* were like a ray of sunshine through the darkness when you came into my life."

The carriage slowed as they turned into the drive for the residence and she sighed as he kissed her one more time and then slid back to his proper place. "We'll have time before supper," she said, dark eyes dancing.

He nodded. "We will. What did you have in mind?"

"Come to my chamber?" she asked, her voice trembling a fraction, as if she weren't certain of his response.

He drew in a long breath. "I would very much like that, Gia."

The carriage stopped and he exited first to help her out. Together they moved into the house, with her greeting the servants gathered there and collecting a few pieces of correspondence waiting there.

"Supper will be at eight, Your Majesty," Livingston said.

She smiled back at Dash. "Good, that will give Mr. Talbot and I time to go over some affairs before I ready myself. Thank you, Livingston."

She exited the foyer, though she slowed her steps so they could go up the staircase together.

"Go over some affairs," Dash repeated under his breath.

She giggled softly. "It isn't untrue, is it? I have one particular affair I'd like to go over at length."

"As do I," he agreed.

They hurried to her chamber and inside the receiving room. He locked the door to grant them privacy and she moved to him in one long step. Into his arms and right back to heated kisses like the ones they'd shared in the carriage. He felt her soften against him, lean into him, surrender all that control she normally had to keep over herself.

He backed her up toward the bedroom, only this time he didn't take her to bed as he had the night before. There was a settee before the fire, and he eased her onto it and took a seat beside her. He cupped her face, slowing his kisses, lingering on every touch so he could savor them in a way he hadn't been capable of the night before.

She moaned against his mouth, reaching for the buttons on his jacket. He pushed her hands away and she drew back, staring at him in concern and question.

"You...you don't want me?" she whispered.

He shook his head. "I want you so much it physically hurts. But you spent the entire day having to serve everyone else around you. I think it's time you relaxed now and let me take control."

CHAPTER 8

Control. There was a loaded word for a woman who always had to maintain it. Sometimes it felt like a bit in her mouth and she had to drag everything in the world forward with it. But Dash was offering her release. Not just in orgasm, but to put down any burdens and just…feel.

"What should I do?" she whispered.

"Lean back on the settee," he said softly. "And trust me."

She slid her hands through his hair one more time, kissed him deeply, then did as he asked, leaning back and watching as he placed a hand on her knee through her gown. Fabric separated them and yet she arched a little at the simple touch.

"You're going to make this too easy," he said on a low chuckle that seem to wend its way through her entire body and settle between her legs.

"Am I?" she asked, continuing to stare as he began to bunch her skirt in his hand, raising it above her knee, up to her thigh. It was a slow, glorious torture and she loved every moment of it.

He nodded. "Yes. Because you respond so quickly to even the lightest of touches. So sensual."

She turned her face. "I've never felt sensual enough when it came to this…to sex."

His brow wrinkled. "Because of him?"

She let out a shuddering sigh. "Yes. Because of him."

Neither of them had to name the *him*, especially after their conversation in the carriage.

"So he was as remiss in his duties to your body as he was to your heart?" he asked.

She shrugged. "I never…hated it. He never hurt me. But he didn't care if he pleased me. And then he just stopped touching me entirely once I had served the purpose of creating his children." She looked at Dash's hand, her skirt bunched in his fingers, his gaze focused entirely on her. "How you make me feel, Dash, is something I have craved a long time."

Dash's expression grew harder, not with desire this time, but with anger, likely long repressed during the years he had served her when her husband still lived.

"King or not, he did not deserve to shine your shoes, let alone touch you," Dash said with a shake of his head. "But knowing that he was so careless with you and your pleasure makes me want to do what I want to do all the more."

He returned his hand to her knee, but this time it was bare skin on bare skin. She made a garbled sound in her throat and twisted toward him, like she could force him to touch her more and more intimately if she just moved the right way.

He rewarded her by sliding his hand to her thigh, pushing her legs open a fraction.

"What do you want to do to me?" she gasped.

"I know what your mouth tastes like," he explained. "And your skin. But I want to know what your desire tastes like, Gia. I want to know what it tastes like when you jolt against me, crying out my name while you come against my tongue."

Her mouth dropped open. Dash was always proper when he spoke to her. She had come to expect it. But now he stared down at her, hands creeping farther beneath her skirt, and he said something so wonderfully wicked that she got wetter just hearing it.

"I want you to taste me," she managed to gasp out. "Please."

She didn't have to ask twice. Not that she ever did with this man. He slid to his knees before her and pushed her legs even wider with his shoulders. She wasn't wearing drawers, just the chemise that he'd been pushing up along with her skirt, so she was bared to him when he opened her wider. She blushed. He'd seen her like this, of course, last night, but now his face was so close to her most intimate of areas.

It was so very wicked.

He leaned in and his beard brushed the inside of her thigh. She lifted against him with a gasp at the rush of sensation. God's teeth, but the man made her wild. He made her feel young and beautiful and erotic. He made her forget everything but the feel of him as he brushed a finger along the length of her sex and smiled up at her when he found her wet.

He didn't say anything, though. He just leaned in and pressed his mouth to her body. It was a gentle kiss at first, closed-mouthed, almost chivalrous except that it was in such an outrageous place. He slid his fingers across her outer lips, massaging the sensitive flesh there as he opened his mouth, and she felt his tongue sweep along her entrance.

"Dash," she cried out in a garbled rush of pleasure and surprise.

He smiled against her as he peeled her open, rubbing even as he licked her with more purpose and pressure. He went on like that, stroking her with his tongue, creating molten heat between her legs and then licking it clean like it was a feast he craved.

She writhed beneath him, stripped of the control he had asked her to surrender as her body rolled with sensation and rapidly building pleasure. His fingers pressed into her thighs and she gasped, his beard abraded her flesh and she lifted against him for more, and his tongue, great God his tongue, did things to her that she had never imagined were possible.

She almost felt she could take no more—he had dragged her to an edge that was on the borderline of pleasure and pain and he held her there with wicked intent, never quite letting her find the release she craved, yet never relinquishing the hold he had on her pleasure.

"Please," she gasped at last. "Dash!"

He looked up at her and it was so very wicked to see him perched between her thighs, her dress bunched around her stomach, him fully clothed as her stockinged legs gripped around his shoulders. A great ripple of pleasure moved through her, and she cried out as her hands flexed against the edge of the settee.

His eyes grew wild, dark with desire and pleasure at her pleasure. He began to suck her clitoris, watching her intently the entire time, holding her captive with his gaze as much as the firm grip he kept on her jolting body.

The pleasure he'd been holding just out of her reach washed over her, rapidly pushing her to the highest heights and then…then the orgasm overcame her with more power than anything she'd ever felt before. She ground against his mouth helplessly, shaking out of control as sensation erased all her thoughts, all her concerns, everything but the man who had created them and was now dragging them out as long as he could.

At last she flopped back, the great heaving waves of pleasure reduced to little earthquakes. He licked her one last time and then shifted higher on his knees, caging her in on the settee as he kissed her and let her taste herself on his slick lips.

She tilted her head, cupping his cheeks as she relaxed into his touch and waited for more. Waited for him to take her once again and even the score of pleasure.

Only he didn't. Instead he smoothed her skirt back down and joined her on the settee, wrapping her in his arms and just…holding her.

She glanced up at him after what felt like an eternity had passed. His eyes were closed, his face entirely at peace. She realized she'd never seen him like this before. He looked softer and younger and oh, so handsome in this calm and serene expression.

"Dash?" she said as she leaned up to kiss the line of his jaw.

He opened his eyes and looked down at her. "Yes?"

"Aren't you going to…" She waved a hand at herself and evoked a laugh from him.

"Take you?" he supplied for her.

She nodded. "I would very much like you to."

His pupils dilated with desire and the corner of his lip quirked with a touch of arrogance. Like he reveled in her wanting him as much as she did the same. "I would very much like to, and I will, Gia. I promise you that. Later."

She sat up. "It doesn't seem entirely fair that you would do something so wonderful for me and not get anything in return."

His brow wrinkled. "Making love to you, giving you pleasure, it isn't a quid pro quo, my dear. I don't count orgasms in a ledger so that they may be even or that I win the race. If someone else did, that is a failing of *his*. Not mine." He leaned forward and kissed the tip of her nose playfully. "Right now I want food. I'm famished after that delightful first course. Aren't you?"

She realized as he spoke that she *was* hungry. "Fine, but I will hold you to your promise that we aren't finished."

"I fully expect you to." He got up and drew her to her feet. Wrapping his arms around her, he kissed her deeply before he stepped away. "I'll see you shortly."

She nodded and watched as he left her chamber, ringing the bell for Betsy as he departed. Because of course he would. The man was built to anticipate her every need, whether it was something benign or shockingly erotic.

She got up from the settee and moved to her mirror. Her eyes were bright, her cheeks pink with high color. She felt giddy with desire and emotion, flush with the first flutters of something wonderful. It was such a strange thing, because she'd known and cared for Dash for so long.

Betsy entered the room and Giabella tried to temper her expression. "Good evening," she said.

"Your Majesty," Betsy said with a small curtsey. "Is it just you and Mr. Talbot for supper, then? I haven't heard anything from household staff."

"I believe so, yes," Giabella said. "But I think I'd still like to wear the teal brocade."

Betsy's brows lifted slightly at her suggestion that she wear the slightly more formal gown for a night with her secretary, but Giabella ignored it. Dash had always complimented her on that gown—she intended to wear it, by God. Use it to add to the anticipation of what would happen after.

She followed Betsy into her dressing area and they began the motions of readying her that they had been repeating for decades. Once she was dressed, she sat and Betsy began to restyle her hair to suit the more formal evening look.

"I've heard all went well with the gatherings today," her maid said, twisting Giabella's hair carefully and pinning it in place.

"I believe so," Giabella said with a smile as she thought of all the wonderful people she had met with.

"The servants who attend to the household full time here have said that they feel the area will support King Grantham in the election, on the whole," Betsy continued.

"That's very good," Giabella said with a sigh. "Of course we had some concern. A population that does not want its king might not want him as a representative for them either. But it does seem the unrest was about the idea of wanting a democracy, not hatred for Grantham specifically."

"Indeed," Betsy agreed. "That is the same thing I've heard over and again. No one could want more than what the king has offered."

"Well, a few might," Giabella said, thinking of Hadley and his anger at the thought of change. Would he bring some kind of hell down on Dash for his physical intervention? And could she protect the man she loved if he did?

"Ma'am?"

Giabella blinked. "I'm sorry, I was woolgathering a moment. What was that?"

Betsy looked at her in the reflection but then said, "I was just wondering what your thoughts were on your own future."

She heard the slight waver to the maid's voice. The worry about her place in the world, since it was so irrevocably linked to Giabella's. And yet she had so few answers to give. Every time she thought of the future, she froze with its vastness. Even more so now that she knew Dash would have a path very much his own to follow.

"I'm not sure," she said slowly. "There will be so much change. But I promise you, Betsy, that you will be taken care of, whether you choose to attend me or not."

"I can't imagine anyone in your private staff leaving you, Your Majesty."

Giabella blinked. Dash's decision to go into the office of the prime minister was not her secret to tell, but Betsy's words made it weigh on her all the more. She heard the ticking of the final clock louder now.

It made her want to cling to the present all the more. Cling to Dash. As long as she could.

~

Dash had changed for supper. Normally he would not, especially when he and Giabella were alone together. A servant did not have the same expectations as a member of the family or someone with exalted position. He was generally nothing more than serviceable in his dress, meant to fade into the background so that everyone looked at Gia.

Not that anyone could ever come into a room and not look at her.

But tonight he had opted for something different. A more formal waistcoat, a sharper edge to his cravat. Being alone with her meant more now. He liked to be able to pretend that they were nothing more than lovers, spending an evening together at their leisure.

Even if that was a lie.

A lie made even more obvious almost as soon as he entered the parlor where he and Gia would have pre-supper drinks. The butler entered, and immediately Dash could see he was needed in his duties.

"I beg your pardon, Mr. Talbot," Livingston began. "But there is a situation."

Dash stepped away from the sideboard and toward the other man. "A situation?" he repeated.

"A visitor has arrived, uninvited, it seems. And I do not know what to do with her."

Dash wrinkled his brow. "*Her*? Who is it?"

"Miss Marabelle Fowler, sir."

Dash drew in a sharp breath. Miss Fowler had once been the leader of the group who had protested Grantham's reign. The very woman who had helped bring about the changes to the government that were about to be put in place. She and the king were working closely together now, and Dash found the young woman to be bright, reasonable and steady. But he kept her away from the queen as much as possible.

Because she was also something else. Something that caused a flicker of hurt in Giabella every time she saw the young woman.

Dash checked the clock on the mantel. Gia would not arrive for another fifteen minutes at the earliest. He had a little time, so he cleared his throat. "Please bring her in."

"Yes, sir." A moment later Livingston was back. "Miss Fowler, sir."

He stepped away and let the young lady into the room. Dash extended a hand as he came to her, looking over her. With her petite frame and dark hair, one might easily overlook the woman. Misjudge her heart or her tenacity. But one look into her piercing blue eyes, the very eyes that caused the pain to Giabella, and it was impossible not to see what a force of nature she was.

"Miss Fowler," Dash said as they shook hands. "Good evening."

"Mr. Talbot," she returned. "You must be surprised to see me. I wager you didn't know I was in the South Island."

"I did not," he confirmed. "May I get you a drink?"

She tilted her head slightly. "So welcoming. I wasn't sure you would be."

He drew back a fraction, both at her charge and her directness. "I...If I have not been in the past, I apologize, Miss Fowler."

She wrinkled her brow. "I haven't entirely expected it, sir. After all, you serve the queen. You protect the queen. And I am not unaware that my existence is something that might...might hurt her."

Dash pursed his lips. "Yes. I won't deny it."

Miss Fowler paced away. "I do not mean to be. My parentage is...it's unfortunate. I know it."

"We are discussing that your father is the late king," Dash said carefully.

"I am his bastard daughter, yes," Miss Fowler said, and without a hint of embarrassment about that fact. "I am fully aware that you normally try to keep me as far from the queen as possible."

Dash opened his mouth to deny it, but couldn't. He thought of the night they had first met this woman, when she had revealed herself as the architect of the work against Grantham. Not the violence, but the very real desire of the people to be ruled by themselves and not a sovereign. Watching Giabella's expression before she had tamed it...

It had broken Dash's heart.

"Perhaps I do," he admitted. "But it doesn't follow that I do not respect you, miss. I do. And I believe the queen feels the same way. No one can deny how hard you have worked for your cause and for our people."

"Thank you." She sighed. "It is because of just that desire to help our people that I have come here tonight. When I heard that the queen was in the area, I thought I'd take a chance and call. I have a matter to discuss with her, you see."

Dash paused to consider the request. As Giabella's secretary, his duty was to ask her what she desired in this situation. As her lover… as one who loved her, he only wanted to shield her from pain, especially when they were enjoying such a beautiful time together.

"What is the matter?" he asked, trying to force himself back into being only the queen's trusted servant.

Miss Fowler shifted, as if now she were a little uncomfortable. "It is something I'd rather talk to Queen Giabella about directly, since it concerns her more than anyone…and also because I do not wish to repeat it more than once."

Dash could see how nervous Miss Fowler was and opened his mouth, ready to get more information, but before he could, he heard Giabella's voice behind him, strained and shaking ever so slightly.

"Miss Fowler," she breathed.

Both of them turned toward her and Dash caught his breath. Giabella had changed into one of his favorite gowns, her hair was arranged just so, and she looked so achingly beautiful that his palms actually itched with the desire to touch her.

But her face…there was that pain that lingered. That humiliation at this living proof of how betrayed she had been in her unhappy marriage.

"Your Majesty," Miss Fowler said, coming forward and giving a deep curtsey. "I am sorry to intrude. It looks as though you might be going out."

Giabella glanced down at herself and blushed. "No, Dash and I were just going to have supper together." Dash was surprised the queen had been so direct in the truth, but it was proof of how thrown she was by the presence of this woman. Miss Fowler glanced back at Dash briefly, her expression unreadable. Giabella continued, "But it sounds as though you have a very serious topic to discuss with me."

"I do," Miss Fowler affirmed. "But only if you would wish to speak to me."

"Of course," Giabella said smoothly and with a kind smile. Of course she would. She was always kind. "Dash, would you tell the staff that we will add one more for our supper plans?"

Dash inclined his head, though he lifted his eyes to snag hers. She nodded ever so slightly, as if trying to tell him that she was fine with this decision even when he saw her hesitation plainly. But he didn't refuse or question her as he excused himself and went to do exactly as she'd asked.

He only hoped that Miss Fowler's topic of discussion would not be one that would crush Giabella's spirit.

CHAPTER 9

Giabella forced a smile for Marabelle Fowler as Dash left them alone. And realized she'd never been alone with the young woman before. Probably by design, now that she thought of it. Her children and Dash had protected her, of course, putting up barricades so she wouldn't have to look into this young woman's eyes and see Alistair. See her own children in the angles of her face and the way she moved and tilted her head.

"You are kind to invite me to supper," Marabelle said, worrying her hands before her. "But I do not wish to intrude."

"You aren't," Giabella said gently, and tried to mean it. "Now, would you like a drink?"

"Sherry would be lovely," Marabelle said.

Giabella crossed to the sideboard and poured them each a drink. When she handed it over, she smiled. "To the future."

Marabelle bent her head and repeated the sentiment. "To the future."

They clinked glasses and then Giabella drew a deep breath and did what she'd been trained to do all her life. She made the young woman comfortable. They talked of books and an art exhibit that had been on display at the Athawick Museum for the past few months. One Giabella had championed. And while she eased Marabelle's conscience, Giabella also found herself relaxing. She actually *liked* this woman. And she had carried far heavier burdens than this one in her life.

She glanced at the clock. "Come, Marabelle, we will go to the dining room."

Marabelle nodded and followed her to the door. As they stepped into the hallway, Giabella saw Dash close to the dining room door, talking to Livingston quietly. Her heart leapt at the sight of him, formal in his clothing like a lover...and yet doing his duties as her employee, her protector.

She lifted a hand and the two men came toward them. She smiled. "Livingston, will you escort Miss Fowler to the dining room and ensure she's settled? Mr. Talbot and I will follow momentarily."

She met Dash's eyes and he nodded.

The butler moved off with Marabelle, and Giabella reached for Dash's hand, threading her fingers through his gently. He shivered at the brush of her bare skin against his and she did the same. This was desire, yes. Shockingly powerful desire at that. But it was also comfort. Such a deep and abiding comfort when he was near her.

"I'm sorry to bring an intruder into what was meant to be our private supper," Giabella said.

He tilted his head and his expression softened as he lifted a hand to brush her cheek. "This seems important," he said. "Of course it would take precedence. Do you wish me to be there? As a buffer?"

She smiled. "I think you are my buffer often enough, aren't you? Always protecting me."

His fingers flexed against her skin and then he dropped them away. "It has been the great pleasure of my life to protect you, Giabella."

"Well, tonight I think I do not need one. Or perhaps shouldn't use one, at any rate. But I do want you to join us, as my friend. As my confidante. As a man who cares for me and one I...I care for." She stumbled over the words, wishing she could make them stronger but recognizing how unfair that was considering the future he was planning for himself.

He smiled down at her. "I am happy to come to your table as all those things, Gia."

She nodded and smoothed her hands down her gown. She glanced back toward the dining room where Marabelle awaited them. "I do fear what she might say with all that anxiety and regret on her expression. But if you're there, I know I can bear it. Let's join her, shall we?"

He motioned for her to lead the way and she did, crossing the hall and entering the dining room. Marabelle was seated on the left of the head of the table and Giabella took that space as Dash placed himself just at her right. If she moved her foot just so, she could let it brush his boot, but didn't.

She needed to focus at present.

The first course was brought out, a shellfish bisque from the fresh catch of the day at the southern port. As they began to eat, the servants left them alone and in that moment, Marabelle set her spoon aside. "You have been kind to be so welcoming, Your Majesty, but I have such anxiety about what I came here to say. Perhaps I might just say it and then you can decide if you wish to evict me from the house."

Giabella sent a side glance to Dash and he frowned. "That sounds very serious, Miss Fowler."

Marabelle glanced at him and nodded. "It is." She drew a long breath. "Your Majesty, I...I fear I have hurt you."

Giabella drew back at that statement. It had not been what she'd been preparing for since she overheard Marabelle's voice in the parlor. "You...you are direct, my dear."

The young woman blushed. "I fear that is true. But I also know that indirectness has also caused both of us to suffer over the years. I wanted to apologize to you for my role in your suffering."

At that Giabella reached out and covered Marabelle's hands. She felt them flex beneath her own and the young woman's eyes went wide as saucers at the action. "Now listen here," Giabella began. "Your parentage is not your fault. You had no control over what my husband did or didn't do any more than I did. You are as much a victim of his flagrant disregard for certain aspects of his duty as I was, so there is no apology necessary."

Marabelle blinked. "Truly? You can be so forgiving?"

"Of course." Giabella sat back. "In truth, I actually admire you. I've watched you work with Grantham over the past few months." She hesitated and glanced at Dash, drawing strength from his steady expression. "Work with...with your brother." Marabelle sucked in a sharp breath at that correction, and Giabella felt Dash lean a little closer at her side even though she didn't look at him. "You are intelligent and tenacious. You think first about your country, just as he does."

To her surprise, Marabelle's blue eyes filled with tears. "Thank you, Your Majesty, for those kind words. For your absolution of my guilt. I have carried it a long while."

"Well, set it down, my dear!" Giabella said with a laugh that she tempered as the second course was brought in.

When the servants had left them again, Marabelle shook her head. "I have enjoyed working with King Grantham, I admit. Helping to shape this new form of government has been satisfying. And exciting, because since we are allowing women to vote, it follows that they will also serve in the future. And my apology precedes my telling you that...that..."

Giabella tilted her head. "You would like to run for a position in the common representation?"

"I would," Marabelle said.

"I think you would be a wonderful addition," Giabella said without hesitation. "And I would give my full support to such a notion if that is what you're asking for."

"Your Majesty," Dash said at her side.

She glanced at him to find him looking evenly at Marabelle and she back at him. The unspoken communication flowing between them was run through with tension. "What is it?"

"Surely you must understand that my coming into such a public space, especially with there still being some grumblings from the nobility about this new form of government, that it might…it might create problems."

"You mean that your parentage might be discovered," Dash said more plainly. He glanced at Giabella. "A man like Count Hadley would take that information and run with it, trying to make it a scandal. Or a way that the royal family is lining the new government with their own operatives."

Giabella flinched at both options. Ones she hadn't thought through in her desire to ease this woman's fears. The second was especially sharp. It was the same reason she could not pursue anything more from Dash than what they were already sharing.

And the scandal…well, Athawick was far more open-minded in their views on sex and passion, but the king's illegitimate daughter would make a stir regardless. People would look at Giabella with… pity, she feared. They would whisper when she entered a room and not because she was queen or former queen.

They would whisper about her husband's mistresses and wonder if there were more children out there with his eyes. She wondered it, after all, even as she tried not to do so. She squeezed her eyes shut at the thought, already feeling the weight of humiliation in her chest.

"Perhaps the queen needs some time to digest this situation," Dash said, sliding back into his role so easily.

"Of course," Marabelle said. "I realize this must be a shock to you. I can leave if you'd like."

Giabella shook her head at that suggestion. "Wait a moment, both of you."

She stared at her plate, trying to reorganize her thoughts. She had so many when it came to Alistair and their long and miserable marriage. Things she pushed down. Buried, because what was the alternative?

"Gia," Dash whispered, and when she dared to look at him she saw how much he wanted to touch her. To comfort her, as if having him at her side wasn't the deepest comfort.

"Alistair was a great many things," Giabella said, slowly returning her stare to Marabelle. "I'm sorry that he was not good to you or to his other children. But my dear, you shouldn't let your future be influenced by your past. You should do what you think is best and not worry about the rest."

Marabelle drew back. "You would be so kind, even though it would also affect you?"

"I would be remiss in denying this country of good leadership for something my late husband did." She smiled at the young woman. "Take your rightful place. You will only find support from the rest of your family, including me."

Marabelle actually sagged with relief and Giabella felt a swell of certainty at her decision. The rest would be dealt with later. But this was right. When she glanced at Dash again, she found him watching her closely, wonder in his gaze. Adoration. Love.

Oh yes, she saw his love for her and her own called back in that charged moment. And for what?

She cleared her throat and forced her official state smile back to her lips. "And now we must talk of less difficult subjects. You were telling me about a book that I think Mr. Talbot would also have great interest in."

Dash leaned forward, but beneath the table she felt the gentle brush of his boot along her slipper. A movement of support and kindness that buoyed her as Marabelle began to talk of other things. And it became a supper of unlikely friends.

And she was able, at least for a little while, to push down all the emotions stirred by this encounter. Ones that she feared would wash over her later.

Marabelle Fowler must have sensed the same thing Dash did about Giabella's fragile state, because she excused herself very swiftly after supper ended. They stood on the front stairs, waving as her carriage moved away. As it disappeared from view around a bend in the drive, Giabella drooped.

He caught her elbow and gently guided her inside. They could have gone to a parlor, of course. Shared drinks like any normal night. Instead, he took her upstairs, back to her chamber. Betsy was in the room as they entered the antechamber. Her expression became concerned as she saw the queen's face.

"Your Majesty?" she murmured, coming forward.

Dash shook his head. "She is fine, Betsy. Just needs a moment. Will you excuse us?"

Betsy gave him a long look and then curtseyed. "I'll be ready for you to ring if you need anything."

Dash flinched as she left. He'd known the maid for over a decade, as long as he'd served Giabella. They had often worked together to ensure the queen's schedule was as easy as possible for her. It was evident Betsy had seen something in him when she looked at him tonight.

He could no longer hide his heart, it seemed.

"I'm sorry," Giabella said softly, detangling herself from his grip and moving across the antechamber to the window, where she looked out into the darkness.

"You need never be sorry," he said. "Not with me."

"No, I suppose not," she said without looking at him. "You have already seen it all. Me at my worst and my best. In grief and in anger. What all the rest of the world has never seen."

"And all it does is prove to me how amazing you are," he said, stepping toward her but not touching her. He didn't want to invade her space in this moment of pain.

She pivoted to face him. "Amazing?" she repeated on a laugh. "I did not feel amazing tonight. I felt…so foolish, Dash."

The tears came into her eyes then and he could no longer stay away. He crossed the rest of the way to her and caught her in his arms, guiding her to the same settee where he had pleasured her earlier in the afternoon. Now he cradled her against his chest there, feeling her breath shake in and out of her.

"Why foolish?" he asked. "Because of your husband?"

"Yes," she whispered against his neck, her warm breath teasing his skin through the folds of his cravat. "Because of the fool my husband made me. Over and over again, sometimes in my own house. Often in the bed I should have shared with him, so I could hear him through the door while I lay awake in the queen's chamber." She drew a shaky breath, harsh memories playing over her face in a picture he hated to see. "And now there is living, walking proof in that remarkable young woman who just left us with all her spark and verve and dreams for a greater future. The one with his eyes."

Dash clenched his jaw. "Gia, if I could have stopped him from hurting you—"

She pushed away slightly and stared up at him. "You couldn't have. And if you had tried he would have had you sacked…or worse." She shivered. "He was an immovable object. And he didn't care who he damaged. In fact, I think he sometimes took pride in it."

Dash took her hands and held them gently between his own. "It was difficult to watch from the sidelines and never do anything."

She pulled one hand from his and placed it against his cheek. "You think you did nothing? Dash, you were my lifeline for ten long years. Your kindness, our connection, they were the little moments I looked forward to each day. And, when he was particularly cruel, the moments that kept me from giving up. You were *everything* to me, wrong as that might have been."

He stared at her. Earlier in the day, Giabella had said she cared for him. A rather tepid sentiment in comparison to the fire of love that he felt for her. But this…this admission was different. And it meant so much that he ached for her.

She lifted toward him. "You've been my fantasy since the first moment I met you, Dash. And I would very much like to fulfill it again."

He nodded as their lips met. It was gentle this time, warm and loving as he slid his fingers into her hair and angled her face to kiss her more deeply. For what felt like a very long time, they just kissed. Like they were young lovers just discovering each other, and he reveled in every soft sigh, in each time her fingers clenched against his forearms.

"Take me to bed," she murmured at last.

He shuddered at the request, his entire body throbbing with the anticipation of doing just that. He got up, drawing her with him, and threaded his fingers through hers. They moved together to the big bed and he turned her around so he could unfasten her dress.

"You look so beautiful tonight," he said, pressing a kiss to the base of her neck, just below her hairline. He breathed her in as he did so, that intoxicating combination of lemon and lavender that always clung to her hair and skin. How many times had he caught it on the air when he leaned in to assist her and wanted to do exactly what he was doing now?

Which was why he had to savor it.

"I wore the dress for you," she admitted, her voice shaky as he slid the gown forward. "You always liked it, didn't you?"

He nodded against her shoulder, pressing light kisses along the line of her body before he looped his fingers under the chemise and drew it down. Together they shoved both dress and undergarments past her hips, and she was naked save her stockings. She slid her slippers off and turned into him, pressing her soft curves against him and finding his mouth.

He let his hands roam, down her sides, over her hips, around to cup her backside and lift her against his rapidly hardening cock.

God, but she drove him wild. Woke some rakish part that he hadn't believed existed in his staid and controlled life.

He found he liked having that hidden part that was only for her. Always for her.

He lifted her to the edge of the bed, nudging between her legs and pressing their bodies even closer. Her fingers went into his hair, she pressed against him with a shudder and her kiss grew wild and heated and raw.

"I need you," she whimpered into his mouth.

He nodded again and stepped back, leaving the warmth of the circle of her arms just long enough to shed his own clothing in record time. She watched him as she pushed herself back on her pillows in the middle of the big bed. Every time he removed an item, her pupils dilated and she shocked him by placing a hand between her legs to touch herself.

He froze, watching her. "God, Gia."

She smiled even as her cheeks pinkened. "I used to think about you when I did this," she admitted. "For years. And then I'd have to come into the parlor the next morning and pretend I hadn't fantasized about your body in mine."

He stripped off the remaining clothing and moved toward her. "What did I do in these fantasies?"

"Everything you have done already," she whispered, continuing to touch herself with one hand while she reached for him with the other. "With your hands, with your tongue, with your cock."

She arched against her fingers, pleasure rippling over her face. Not quite an orgasm, but something very close. He took a place next to her and placed his hand over hers, joining her to stroke her sex. She was slick already. She turned her head into his throat, sucking gently as she lifted into him, into herself. Together they worked at her and when she came, she groaned into his skin, like she could pour that pleasure between them as she arched against their fingers.

He urged her to her side, her back to his chest, and aligned himself against her entrance. She pushed back, taking him before he could make the same move, and he chuckled at her ardor. A sound that faded into a moan as her heated sex gripped him. He fully seated himself and began to gently grind. Her body still twitched with her orgasm and he loved the fluttering around his cock. He wanted it again. He wanted to take her control, give her nothing but sensation to erase a difficult night.

She rocked back against him, his name echoing from her lips over and over again as he took her in long, slow strokes. He wrapped his arm around her body, threading their fingers together while he took. She leaned into him, her gasping breaths coming shorter and shorter.

He put her hand back between her legs and she glanced over her shoulder at him, question in her eyes. He held that stare. "Come for me. Come all around me. I want to feel it."

Her pupils dilated to almost fully black and she began to grind against her own hand. The grip of her sex intensified, tighter and wetter as she increased her own pleasure. It increased his, as well, and he gripped her hip hard enough that he dented her flesh. Sensation streaked up his cock, settled in his balls, a slow build to an explosion he knew would be harder and hotter and more powerful than the last.

She gasped and he felt her strokes become more erratic, the edge of release. When she fell, it was a cacophony of sensation as she ground back against him, crying out in the quiet, her body gripping his so hard that he couldn't control himself anymore.

He moved to pull from her, but she pressed back harder. "In me," she gasped. "Please!"

He couldn't deny her, nor himself, any longer, and he poured into her with a guttural, animal cry. He stroked so hard as he came that he pushed her partly on her stomach, rising over her as they came together and then collapsed, him partly covering her, their sweat mingling.

At last he found the strength to roll away from her and she turned to face him, snuggling against his side with a satisfied sigh.

"Did I just utterly defile a queen?" he asked, staring down at her.

She laughed as she looked up at him. "By coming inside of me?"

He nodded.

"If you did, I would want nothing less than to be defiled. After all, I am past the age of bearing children, so there is no risk to it. And I liked feeling you inside me when you spent."

He shivered at her directness and the images it created. And if he weren't exhausted by having her, he might have gone right back to the act. But instead he gathered her closer and kissed her temple. "I liked everything about what we did, Gia. And if you give me an hour, I'll like it all over again."

She giggled, an almost girlish sound that reflected no worries, no pains, and he felt a satisfaction the likes of which nothing else had ever given him. Because he had helped her, and that was, in the end, the greatest duty of his life.

Even if it couldn't always be.

CHAPTER 10

Giabella had always been able to compartmentalize herself when it came to her duties. Whether she was having a good or bad day personally, she could enter a room filled with dignitaries or subjects and dazzle as a good queen should. No one could ever read her expression if she didn't allow it.

But today, standing in the middle of the receiving room, surrounded by ladies and gentlemen for her farewell tea before their return to the capital, she was…distracted. The reason was, of course, Dash, who stood across the room, talking to Count Friskar.

He was so handsome that her heart fluttered like a schoolgirl's. And when he glanced her way and gave just the slightest of supportive smiles, that heart throbbed all the more powerfully.

"Your Majesty?"

Giabella blinked and returned her attention to the companion she had all but forgotten was at her side. Lady Allen, one of the lesser gentry from the central part of the island, and a woman who had always been someone she counted as a friendly acquaintance.

"I'm sorry, my dear," Giabella said, and felt her cheeks heating. "I found myself distracted."

"Understandably," Lady Allen said with a warm smile. "You must have so much on your mind with the election just weeks away. And then…what? Have you put much thought into your future?"

Giabella glanced again at Dash. She knew him so well after all this time, she could parse out even the slightest hint of his mood or thoughts. He was in his element at the moment, talking to Friskar as something closer to an equal than he ever had as a servant. That is what a position in government would give to him: a higher footing that he certainly deserved.

And a future she refused to disrupt, even if it broke her heart. After all he'd given her? She couldn't.

"I've been thinking a great deal of Everlay lately," she said after a pause. "My old homeland is a place I've not visited in years, and I was never able to have an extended stay when I went. Perhaps after everything settles, that would be the…the best decision for me. And for the country."

"How so?" Lady Allen asked, her brow wrinkling.

Giabella sighed. "The last thing this country will need is reminders of the monarchy they are about to reject lurking around every corner, spending their money and potentially influencing decisions despite the election." She tried to avoid looking at Dash yet again. Almost impossible. He was a magnet for her. An irresistible pull. "I want everyone to have a chance to settle into their new roles before I make myself a regular public figure again."

Lady Allen nodded slowly. "I would miss you, of course. Your lovely company is always a pleasure. But I understand the desire. It is admirable, really. All of what your family is surrendering is admirable. I hear it from the people regularly when I am out and about in the world. They want their freedom, their autonomy, but they do not hate you."

"Most of the time power must be removed through violent means," Giabella said with a shiver. "That Grantham was willing to simply surrender it is something I am very proud of. I hope that the others in control will feel the same and not act out of malice."

Lady Allen tilted her head. "Are you talking about Lord Hadley? About the altercation between you a few nights ago?"

Giabella jerked her attention to her friend. "What do you know about that?"

"People talk," Lady Allen said with a cluck of her tongue. "You know that better than most. I've heard, though, that he is sorry for what he did. I believe he was in his cups, perhaps more deeply than he appeared at the party that night."

Giabella pursed her lips. "Do you think his regret is sincere?"

Lady Allen shrugged. "I've known the man most of my life. My father thought to match me with him once." She pulled a face. "Can you imagine? But while I think he can be pompous and ridiculous… I do think he is mostly harmless. And he is intelligent enough to know when he is beaten. So yes, I think he regrets doing something that might make an enemy of someone who in the last few days has proven herself to be so very loved by our people."

Giabella pondered that. She was diplomatic enough to know that making an enemy, even one who deserved it, wasn't always the best course. She touched Lady Allen's hand. "You must excuse me, Lady Allen. I have something to attend to."

"Of course. I will see you in the capital in a few weeks anyway, for the official surrender of the crown. And hopefully…very likely from what I hear…the triumphant declaration that King Grantham will transform into prime minister."

"One hopes," Giabella said with a smile before she slipped away to find the closest guard. She had a message to send. One that could be a final act as queen to protect her son, her kingdom, and the man she loved more than anything.

The afternoon reception had ended half an hour before, but Dash had not seen Giabella since she said farewell to her last guests and excused herself to rest for a while. He had thought to join her, but there was something about her demeanor that had held him off. She needed a little time to relax by herself, he thought, before they spoke of their travel plans for the next few days and then spent a final night in this place together.

He passed by Livingston in a parlor and circled back, poking his head through the door. "Livingston, have you seen Her Majesty?"

The butler lifted his head and nodded. "Indeed, sir. She is in the blue parlor with Lord Hadley."

Dash's mouth dropped open before he could control the reaction. "Hadley!" he barked, far sharper than he should have.

Livingston's confused expression gave proof to how odd the reaction seemed. "Yes, sir. She requested his presence midway through the party, to join her when the rest had gone. He arrived… ten minutes or so ago?"

"Bollocks," Dash grunted, pivoting on his heel and heading toward the blue parlor.

"Sir, she asked not to be disturbed!" Livingston called out behind him.

Dash ignored it, of course. As her secretary, he ought not. He ought to trust the queen to handle her own business and the guards to manage things if she could not.

But as her lover, as one who loved her, he couldn't do as she requested. And he couldn't tamp down the frustration and confusion about the fact that she hadn't told him of her plans. That was as terrifying as the fact that she was with a person who had manhandled her just a few nights before.

He reached the parlor and threw open the door, storming in blindly, at the ready for whatever he would find there. Giabella and Hadley were seated across from each other, tea between them on the low table. When he burst into the room, they both looked up at him in surprise.

"Dashiell," Gia said, her gaze darting from his. He saw her guilt, though, that she had kept this meeting a secret. "I was not expecting you to join us."

"Probably because I was not informed of the meeting, Your Majesty," he said, trying to calm his racing heart as he looked at Hadley. The man looked...chastened. Which was an odd enough thing as it was. He certainly did not look like a threat.

"An oversight," Gia said weakly. She cleared her throat. "I was...I asked Lord Hadley here to clear up the unfortunate misunderstanding we had a few nights ago."

Hadley glanced up at Dash, and at least there was a flicker of fear in the man's eyes. It seemed his punch had landed in more than one way. "Er, yes. I was so pleased to hear from you. And as I had started to say before we were interrupted, I wanted to apologize for my bad behavior that night."

Dash's eyes went wide and he glanced at Gia. She gave him a meaningful look and he sat down hard in the chair next to Hadley's, watching as the queen...*his* queen...worked her magic.

"I appreciate that. Do continue," she said, regal as she'd ever been.

Hadley shifted like a child being brought to task. Not the worst comparison. "I was in my cups and behaved badly. I should never have spoken to you in such a fashion, nor ever touched you."

Giabella inclined her head. "Thank you, my lord. Your sentiments are very happily received. I think in these trying times of change, any one of us could find the bounds of our behavior... frayed. I accept your apology."

Dash pursed his lips. He would not have accepted what had been said so easily, especially considering this man's past involvement with troubling figures.

He cleared his throat and Giabella lifted a brow. "Mr. Talbot, do you have something you would like to add?"

"I do, Your Majesty," he said, and turned toward Hadley. "Your involvement with the disgraced and deceased courtier, Blairford, is not under dispute. He admitted as much, including that he hoped to install you as king after a murderous coup."

The color drained from Hadley's cheeks, though Dash wasn't

certain if it was because the man had been caught at a plot or was horrified to hear he had been associated with one. Dash continued, "The reason this has not been brought up is a benefit of the doubt the royal family wished to give to you, especially during such times of change. But after what occurred a few nights ago, I would be remiss in my duties if I didn't bring it up. Do you deny your involvement in such a dastardly plan?"

Dash didn't expect the man to admit he was involved, but he wished to see the way it was denied. Hadley shook his head, his lower lip trembling. "Sir, Your Majesty, I assure you I was not in any way aware of such a terrible thing."

Giabella tilted her head. There was a steeliness in her eyes, one Dash knew had been born the same moment he'd been shot. That she hid it was because she was very good at being queen, nothing else. "And yet you were involved with Blairford," she said in an icy tone that dared the man to lie.

"I...was," he admitted, and Dash drew back in surprise. "Blairford had the same opinions that I did, that the uprising of the people was not good for...for..."

"The nobility?" Dash pressed. "For your own pocket and position?"

He could see his interjection annoyed Hadley as the man shifted in his seat and tried desperately not to glare. "Something to that effect," he said through clenched teeth. "Yes. But I assure you that I had nothing to do with a murder plot or a coup." He hesitated. "But I can see why you would fear that, Your Majesty."

Giabella rose slowly, and that forced Dash and Hadley to do the same. She looked at the count, her gaze narrow, and said, "I do hope that you are telling the truth, my lord. Because although we may not always...always like change, to fight against it is folly. The best thing you can do is accept what is going to happen. And find your place in it." She motioned to the door. "Thank you for clarifying and for your apology."

Hadley glanced toward where he was being dismissed and

nodded. "Yes, Your Majesty. Please assure the king that I will be at the capital for all the festivities and I shall not cause any trouble."

"Of course," Giabella said coolly. "Good night."

"Good night," Hadley said with a low bow and then a nod for Dash before he raced from the room, as if he wished to escape before he was caught up by the hounds of hell themselves.

Giabella smiled as they heard the count depart the house and then turned to Dash. "Well, what do you think, Dash? Was he telling the truth?"

He stared at her, his hands beginning to shake as the weight of what she'd done settled on him once again. He said nothing but moved to the parlor door.

"Dash?" she repeated, concern in her turn.

He yanked the door shut with a bang and then pivoted on her. "What I think, Gia, is that you just endangered yourself in the most foolhardy way. And I have no idea why you would *ever* do such a thing."

Giabella took a long step back as Dash stared at her, face bright with...with *anger*. He had never shown anger toward her, not in all their years together. She wasn't certain whether to welcome it as a reflection of their deepening intimacy or to lash back in defense.

"Why are you upset?" she asked, trying to maintain the cool calm she had trained into herself over the years. It was far harder with this man.

"Why am I upset?" he repeated, taking a long step toward her. "You went behind my back and you invited to a private meeting a man who *assaulted* you not three nights ago."

She drew a breath. "He grabbed my arm, Dash, let us not over-state it."

"He *manhandled* you," Dash said, his voice wavering a fraction.

"And he could have easily done something worse tonight when you invited him into a parlor alone without me."

She blinked at the fire in his stare. The fear for her. "Dash...there is always a guard just outside the door."

"And a guard might not get here soon enough," he insisted. "Why in the world would you do something like that, Gia?"

"Do you not know why?" Giabella asked, tilting her head. "Oh, I could tell you it was for Grantham's sake. Or to ease the tension between the aristocracy and the crown as the transition takes place. Both those answers seem very palatable. But the truth is that I...I did it for you."

His face twisted in what seemed like horror. "For *me*?"

"You struck him when he touched me," she said softly.

"After he touched you, a far greater crime," he reminded her.

She shrugged. "But he still might have harbored resentment for months, even years. If he was not addressed by someone of royal blood, by me, then he could have...he could have brought hell down on you eventually. He could have hurt you politically, even physically. I was trying to protect you."

He did not speak for nearly thirty seconds, just stared at her as if she had sprouted a second head or spoken some language he didn't understand. Then he ran a hand through his hair and turned away from her. "Protecting me is not your occupation, Gia. Protecting you, seeing to your every need, is mine."

The words hit her like a slap. She stared at his back as she tried to find words, find breath. "Is that all this is to you, Dash? An occupation? A duty?"

He pivoted to face her. "A duty, yes. And a pleasure always."

She shook her head. "You do not see us as equals," she whispered.

"We are *not* equals," he answered, just as softly. "We never will be, even if we pretended during these wonderful stolen days of ours."

She felt the sting of tears behind her eyes, the tightness to her throat as she stepped away from him. *Pretended*...as if this were just some fantasy that had ended, because he'd used the past tense to describe it. And perhaps it was better at that, since she knew that their future together was so very limited.

"Well, I would not wish for you to be forced to pretend any longer, Dashiell," she said. "If you feel it is not my place to protect you, if you cannot see us as equals, then I fear I have put you in a very bad position. And it is likely best if we leave it at that."

She turned away, praying with every step that he would call her back. Drag her back. That he would take her into his arms and tell her they could find a way, a path that she just couldn't see on her own. Even if it weren't true, at least she would know that they were in this boat together, sailing into the storm they couldn't avoid.

But he didn't. In the end, as she reached the parlor door and opened it, all he did say was, "Good night."

So she left, staggering back to her room, locking herself in for something she rarely allowed herself: a long cry. She had earned it, after all.

CHAPTER 11

Dash had chosen to ride in the carriage with Giabella the next day. Partly because that was his place, but mostly because he had missed her so very much the night they'd spent apart and he'd hoped he could talk to her now that emotions had cooled. But she had been the queen when he got into the vehicle the next morning. She had been the queen all day, his passionate lover and dearest friend packed away with all her gowns and tiaras for the ride home.

And so he had allowed for it. He had spoken to her about itineraries and plans, reviewing not just the next two days of travel, but also the next few weeks of events leading up to the first election in the country. She had nodded and given direction when he had questions and been positively polite.

And it had driven him mad all day.

Now the afternoon waned and she looked out the window listlessly, her expression far away as the rig began to slow while they made their way into the village of Corkgrove, just below the royal residence of Menington where they had stayed their first night of this tour what felt like a lifetime ago. Where they'd first kissed on the beach and changed everything between them.

She waved, smiling at her people through the window even if it didn't quite meet her eyes. Eyes she darted toward him.

"Dash," she said softly, continuing to greet her subjects as they cheered along their route.

"Yes?" he said, setting the papers in his hands down to fully focus on her.

"This is our last night on this tour," she said. "Our last night alone together before we return to the whirlwind that will encompass the next few weeks. And then all the changes that will follow." She did look at him then. "And whatever else has happened, I do not wish to waste this last night together. Before this is truly over."

His breath caught and relief washed over him. "I don't want to waste one moment with you," he agreed. "And if you want me tonight, I am yours."

She flinched ever so slightly at his wording. "I intend to take supper in my chamber after a bath. Will you come to me at seven?"

He nodded. She was still distant, but he would take what he could get. Tonight he could show her how much she meant to him and perhaps that would close the gap that had been created by the argument the night before. "Yes. Of course."

"Good," she said, smoothing her clothing as the carriage entered the residence gates and came to a stop at the top of the drive. "I…" She leaned across and took his hand, her lower lip trembling ever so slightly. "I do want you so very much, Dash. I need you."

He lifted her hand to his lips and gently caressed her knuckles. When a shiver worked through her entire body, he whispered, "I need you, too, Gia."

The carriage rocked slightly as the servants disembarked and Gia released his hand, setting hers back in her lap. When the door opened and one of the footmen extended a hand into the rig to help her exit, she sent Dash one last smile. Then she was gone, bustling into the residence, talking to the servants, reuniting with Betsy, who had gone ahead that morning and was already waiting for her.

Dash sighed. He could feel the pull of being parted already.

Parted permanently this time, thanks to the role he would take in the government.

And he had never felt so empty.

Giabella looked around the bedroom and drew a sigh of relief. No one could say it didn't look beautiful, with dozens of lit candles on every surface and a bright fire burning to warm the room. Her bed was turned back, ready for what would come next. And she was in her prettiest nightrail, a beautiful contraption of pale pink silk and lace and perfectly tied bows at her shoulders.

Betsy must have known what she was planning when she helped Giabella prepared the room. She had a sense that the maid was more than aware of all her activities in the last week or so. But she said nothing and simply helped her, then left her to her waiting.

The clock in the hall struck seven and there was a rap on her door at the exact moment. She smiled. Dash, on time as usual. As predictable in that way as the clock itself.

"Come in," she called, loud enough that it could be heard through the antechamber and the door.

She heard him open it, heard him enter. Her heart began to race as he moved through the other room and then stepped into the entrance of the bedchamber. He came to a sudden halt as he stared at her, standing beside the bed, ready for him.

"My God," he breathed.

She looked him up and down. He was wearing dark trousers, a crisp white shirt rolled to the elbows and black suspenders, but no waistcoat, no jacket. His lightly graying hair was tousled, like he'd been running his hands through it as he waited for their agreed upon meeting time, but every other part of him was perfectly in place.

He looked utterly delicious.

"That nightgown is…" He trailed off and licked his lips.

She smiled and edged to stand before the fire, where she knew her body would be outlined by the flames through the thin silk. "Do you like it better now?"

"I'll like it better when it's rumpled on the floor," he said, and moved toward her in a few long steps. She met him halfway and they collided, as if they had been kept apart for weeks, not just one night. Their mouths met, hungry and desperate...oh yes, it was desperate, their last night together...and his hands bunched against the back of her gown as she gripped one of his suspenders in her fist.

"We could talk about—" he began.

She shook her head. "No talking. Just taking. Please."

There was a moment when she thought disappointment flashed in his eyes, but then it was gone, replaced by desire as he pushed her back onto the bed and pushed between her legs. The nightrail bunched between her legs and she gripped his hips with her thighs as he claimed her mouth once more.

His mouth moved down her throat, tracing the line there with his tongue, then lower as he tugged the straps of her nightgown away. She arched into him as he latched his mouth onto one nipple, sucking and swirling his tongue there in a lazy rhythm meant to tease and pleasure her. It worked. She moaned softly, unable to resist as he dropped her back against the mattress. His mouth dropped lower, dampening the silk of her nightdress as he smoothed it along her stomach, her hip. He hitched up the fabric and then he was between her legs.

She lifted against him as he sucked her clitoris, immediately taking her to the edge where he dangled her as he licked and sucked and swirled. She met him stroke for stroke, gripping the mattress edge as he tormented and teased for what felt like an eternity. Only when she was flushed with want, only when she was begging him for release did he give it. He focused his attention on her swollen clitoris, fingering her gently until she came in a gasping cry and twisted against him as the waves wracked her.

When it was over, she caught his shoulders and urged him up, kissing him and tasting her release on his slick lips. "More," she whispered, whimpered.

He nodded against her and stepped back to remove his clothing. She shrugged from her nightgown and was about to slide from the side of the bed onto the pillows, but he held up a hand. "No, wait there."

She did as she'd been told, watching as he stripped naked and appreciating every bit of the view. Appreciating it more as he came back to her, his hard cock lifted against his belly. When he kissed her this time, she took him in hand, stroking over and over until he grunted with pleasure.

"Roll over," he said, breathless.

She arched a brow, but did as she'd been asked. Now she was bent over the edge of the bed and she smiled as what he wanted became clear. She spread her legs wider, going up on her tiptoes to offer the best angle at her body.

He took her in one long stroke, his fingers digging into her hips as he claimed her hard and fast. She burrowed her fingers between her thighs, stroking in time until they both cried out and her orgasm milked him through his.

They collapsed together and lay there for a moment before she laughed. "I think I might not be young enough to hang half off a bed all night."

"Indeed, neither am I," he said with a chuckle of his own. He moved away from her and they took their more comfortable place on the pillows, her legs tangled in his, his hand running through her hair gently. After a short while, he drew a long breath. "Are you certain you don't want to talk about…about everything?"

She squeezed her eyes shut at the question. At the pain it generated. She glanced up at him and their eyes met and held. "What is there to talk about?" she asked. "What is there to say that won't hurt each other? You said something last night, that these were stolen moments. And I treasure every one of them I got to take. And now we will go to the future, our individual futures, and we'll never have to wonder what this would have been like. What we missed out on."

He wrinkled his brow as if he didn't fully agree with that sentiment, but she felt the surrender in his body language even before he said, "As you wish, Gia."

It should have made her happy that he wasn't going to fight her or insist on some long and drawn-out conversation that would only end in more heartache. But she somehow wasn't. A fight wasn't what she wanted, but when he didn't insist upon one, everything felt so final.

He must have sensed it too, because he lifted up a little, staring down at her. "We leave after dawn tomorrow, Gia. And if you'd let me, I'd like to use every moment we have left until then."

She nodded as she reached up and wound her hand against the back of his neck. "I want nothing less than every single moment we have left, Dash."

They came together again, this time with more gentleness, with more of a hint of regret behind the passion. And she tried to forget herself in his touch, his kiss, one last time.

CHAPTER 12

The arrival back in the capital was one of great fanfare and celebration, and Dash had to let Giabella go as she made her way through family and friends. He supposed that was always the end of this: letting her go. But watching her now as she stood with King Grantham and Queen Ophelia, talking close about her trip, he had never felt further from her.

Time was running out for them. It had already run out in some respects. They certainly couldn't do the same things they had been doing right here in the palace with Giabella's children a few doors down from her own rooms.

No, she was back to being queen mother. And he was back to being her secretary, at least for a few more weeks. And he would savor that until he had nothing left.

As the king kissed his wife's hand then left the room and Giabella stepped away from the rest, she arched an eyebrow toward Dash and he moved to her side. "Yes, Your Majesty?"

She flinched ever so slightly at that return to formality. "The princesses and Queen Ophelia have arranged for a luncheon, and I believe the king wishes to speak to you if you have a moment."

He glanced toward the door where Grantham had departed. "Of

course. Shall we meet again later to discuss tomorrow's meeting about the decorations for the dissolution of the crown?"

She inclined her head. "Yes, I believe Ophelia wishes to have that discussion after supper. Why don't you arrange it with her staff?"

She gave him one last meaningful look and then moved to her daughters-in-law with a wide smile. "Have I overheard you two talking about that wonderful pork loin as the main course for lunch? You do know it's my favorite."

They all left the room together, laughing and chatting, in high spirits. Dash took a moment alone in the room, drawing a long breath. And that was that. She was off now, out of his reach again. Likely forever.

He tried to ignore the pain of that fact and smoothed his jacket before he headed down the hallway toward the king's study. He knocked on the partly open door and Grantham's voice responded from within. "Come."

Dash stepped inside and found the king not at his desk, but at the window, staring out toward the garden where the ladies were gathering. He had a soft smile on his face, the one he seemed to reserve for Ophelia. In that moment, Dash felt a harsh stab of jealousy.

Grantham could have the future he desired. And Dash? Well…

"You look dreadfully serious," Grantham said as he faced Dash with an arched brow. "Odd considering I've heard from reports from the road that your travels were a smashing success."

Dash wrinkled his brow. "Reports from the road, Your Majesty?"

Grantham tilted his head. "If you do not think I have spies everywhere, you understand the monarchy less than I believed."

Dash shifted. Good Lord, what those spies could potentially have reported. He might not have a position to come into if Grantham found out what was happening with Giabella.

"Sit, won't you?" Grantham said, motioning to the seat across from the desk. He took his own place, steepling his fingers against the wood. "Tell me about the situation in the south."

Dash drew a breath of relief and quickly recounted what he had observed. Grantham listened closely, asking pointed questions that got to the heart of the matter. And when they were finished with the topic, the king looked pleased.

"Thank you," Grantham said. "I'm pleased that the situation is calming and that support is high for the new government in the most cantankerous area."

"You're held in loving regard, Your Majesty," Dash said. "As is your mother, of course."

Grantham snagged his gaze and held there. "Yes. My mother. Shall we discuss the topic of my mother?"

Dash swallowed. "She did well, as always. She even brought Hadley to his knees."

A flicker of a smile twitched across Grantham's lips, but faded swiftly. "And what about the two of you?"

Dash forced himself to hold the king's gaze. "I'm not sure what you mean."

"I have heard you two grew…closer…during this trip, Dash," Grantham said softly. "Would you care to address that?"

Dash gripped the armrests of his chair. "Are you asking as my king? My employer? Or as a son?"

"I don't think I can parse out the differences at present," Grantham said. "So I ask as all three."

"To the king, I would say that your mother did nothing that would ever bring shame to the crown, for so long as it lasts, and comported herself with as much grace as always. As your employee, I would remind you that I still work for the office of the queen, not the king. And if the position we discussed recently is still offered to me, I do not think I would be seen as an employee anymore. So my actions are not directed by you either way."

Grantham was staring at him, but there was a twitch of a smile on his face rather than anger at his impertinence.

Dash drew a long breath. "And to her son…well, know that I would never hurt her." He pondered Giabella's obvious pain with this entire situation and shook his head. "I would never *purposefully* hurt her."

"Fair points, all," Grantham said, leaning back in his chair. "And I suppose you are trying to tell me that whatever is between you is none of my business. Which is true. Except that I adore my mother. I watched her suffer for decades. I would like to see her happy. And since I asked as a son, not just to her…but to…to you."

Dash's eyes went wide.

"Yes, I mean what I say," Grantham said. "You were always far more of a father figure to all of us than the man who shared our blood. And so I look to your happiness as much as hers when I pry. Did you two get closer?"

Dash nodded slowly. "Yes."

"Good," Grantham said. "Then the plan worked."

"The plan?" Dash repeated. "You're saying you hoped that we would…we would…"

He didn't know how to describe what had happened in an appropriate way and was pleased when Grantham held up a hand. "Let's just keep calling it grow closer. For my sake, as much as yours."

"Fine," Dash said. "You were hoping your mother and I would *grow closer*?" He made a face. "This is not a conversation I ever hoped to have with you."

Grantham snorted a laugh. "Nor I you. I honestly hoped that over the last six months you two might have worked it out for yourselves. And yet you haven't, and with things about to change, I thought a little push might be in order."

Dash ran a hand through his hair. "I appreciate your kind words. I appreciate when you tell me that I have been a father in your life. I care deeply for your family."

"And you love my mother." Grantham said it as a fact, not a question.

"But in many situations love is not enough," Dash said softly.

"I've served her, and she may not have a title as queen after the election, but she will always be queen to those around her."

"But you will not remain a servant." Grantham leaned forward. "Taking the position in my government will put you two on more even footing, Dash."

Dash wrinkled his brow. "Is that why you did it? To give us some chance?"

Grantham shrugged. "I did it because you will be the best man for the job. But the fact that it will even things with my mother is an added bonus."

"I talked to her about the position," Dash said. "It did not seem to influence her thoughts on her future. She views whatever happened between us as a temporary thing. And it is over now. The fact is that I doubt I would ever be worthy of her, whether I am minister of the interior or secretary to the queen."

"That is bollocks," Grantham said. "Cowardly foolishness, Dashiell, and I am shocked to hear you say it. If you refuse to pursue a future with her, it is because of some other reason, but not worthiness. No one in this family believes you anything but worthy, including my mother. You are her dearest friend, her truest confidante, and now that I have experienced love of my own, I can recognize you are the love of her life."

Dash's heart went to his throat at that observation. One that caused him pain as much as joy. Terror as much as exhilaration. Certainly, she was the love of *his* life.

Grantham let out a long sigh when Dash didn't answer. "I am intruding where I should not. I knew it when I sent you away together, I know it now. But I almost threw away a chance at my own happiness." He glanced toward the window again, as if he could see Ophelia in his mind's eye. His tone was rougher when he said, "And I think both you and my mother deserve better than to regret what you didn't pursue. At least think about it. Think about how empty your life, her life, will be if you let her go."

Dash bent his head. What Grantham said was exactly what he

had been avoiding thinking about. But now it sat on his chest, a weight that he felt through every limb and nerve and vein.

"I will," he said softly, and pushed to his feet. "Is that all, Your Majesty?"

"For now," Grantham said, and stood, extending a hand over the desk. "Dash."

Dash shook the offered hand, feeling Grantham's warmth toward him, his sincere regard. And he sighed as he left the room and headed to his own. To ponder. To think. And to make the greatest decision of his life.

~

Giabella sat at the supper table, surrounded by her laughing family. She smiled along with them, but her gaze kept slipping down to the opposite side of the table where Dash sat.

He'd been watching her all night, his blue gaze unreadable and yet piercing into her soul. Something had changed in him since their arrival back in the capital. More than just a return to their duties and positions.

"—go to Everlay," Priscilla was saying.

Giabella blinked at the mention of her home country and looked at her daughter-in-law. "I'm sorry, my dear, what were you saying?"

Priscilla looked at her with a little confusion but repeated herself. "I was just saying that Remi suggested we take a trip to Everlay after everything settles. Perhaps in the autumn. I've heard so much of your home country, Mama. I do long to see it."

Giabella nodded. "And the autumn is a lovely time to go. You could stay at my residence there, Blythe House."

Priscilla shot a side glance toward her husband. "Is that the place where you—"

Remi's eyes went wide and he held up a hand. "No, no, what happens in Everlay should very much stay in Everlay, my dear. My mother does not want to discuss things I did at Blythe House."

Giabella arched a brow at him. Remi had been so wild until Priscilla came into his life. She knew of quite a few parties that her youngest son had partaken in and she certainly didn't want to discuss them.

"Well, perhaps I shall accompany you," she said, refusing to glance down the table at Dash. "After all, once the election is held and the power is transferred, it might be a good thing for the royals to make themselves scarce. I don't want anyone ever thinking I was influencing this government from the sidelines. It seems like something your father would do."

Grantham wrinkled his brow from the head of the table. "Mama, I do not think anyone would ever accuse you of such."

She did look at Dash now. "They might under the wrong circumstances. And…" She drew in a long breath. "I've been considering my future even more the last few days. I thought…I thought I might make my permanent residence Blythe House, at least for the next few years."

The table fell to shocked silence except for the clatter of Dash's fork as he dropped it against his plate. She jerked her gaze to his, finding his eyes wild and wide as he stared at her.

"Mama…" Remi began, all humor gone from his expression.

Dash didn't allow him to continue. He pushed to his feet, his chair screeching against the hard wood as he did so. He stared at her and the room stared at him in return. He opened and shut his mouth twice. "You would leave Athawick," he choked out at last, his tone shaky and uncertain.

She swallowed. This was not how she should have done this, but telling him privately seemed far too difficult. Doing it once, just once, felt better. Except now, after she'd done it, it felt so much worse. He had absolutely no color in his cheeks.

"It might be the best for all involved," she said softly, "for me to create distance."

"It has nothing to bloody do with all involved," Dash said. "Be honest, Gia. You are doing this to create distance from *me*."

Grantham was up on his feet instantly and without a word he motioned to the dining room door. En masse the entire family hustled out, leaving their half-eaten meals behind. Giabella blushed as Priscilla shut the doors behind them with a quick glance her way. Great God, now it was all out. They all had to know something had changed between her and Dash. They would all have their opinions soon enough.

And yet none of that mattered as much as Dash. He moved along the opposite side of the table, coming toward her, even though there was still that barrier of furniture between them.

"Answer me," he said.

She choked on a gasp and then gathered herself. "Yes. Yes, I would leave because of you."

He turned his head. "Gia."

"Not because of anything we did or shared, not because you've done anything wrong. You've never done anything but the right thing, my dearest Dash. But you have a chance at a real future, something just for you that you deserve so much. And if I stay, I will only be in the way of it. Because I know in my heart that I will want to be near you. And you will always turn toward me. I'll interfere in your work, I'll make this entire government suspect and I will…I'll hate myself for keeping you from what and who you were meant to be."

He fisted a hand at his side, his frustration clear on his face. "God, the two of us. Always trying to protect each other and never directly talking about the thing between us. Habit, I suppose. One we never changed even when your husband was gone and we could have been honest." He shook his head. "I must be honest now, though."

"Honest about what?" she whispered.

"Why do you think I decided to take a position in this government?"

"To give yourself a remarkable opportunity, to impact the future of our country. To do more than simply carry around my paperwork and remind me the names of some titled fop's four sons so that I might make that man feel important."

"I did it because I…I love you, Gia."

Giabella got up slowly, her limbs feeling numb as his words pierced the very heart of her. "What did you say?"

"I love you, Giabella," he repeated. "God, I have held those words in for fifteen years. I could have said them the first moment I met you and known they were true and would be true for the rest of my life. Every single thing I did and said to you was the I love you I couldn't speak. And I have regretted none of it. I have never wanted for more than to stand at your side and make your life better and happier."

"Then…then why take the position with Grantham?"

"Because I thought it a way to raise myself. Never to your level, of course, I knew it could never be to your level. But something closer to it. So I had something better to offer. And so that I wouldn't be a member of your staff since that is…tricky when it comes to also being your lover."

She reached up to cover her lips. "Dash."

"Could you love me, Gia?" he asked, and now he moved again, coming around the table to her side, drawing her away from the table, closer to the fire, holding both her hands in his. "Don't protect me anymore, just tell me the truth of what could be in your heart."

"I love you already," she admitted, and her heart almost soared as she let that truth free at last. "I have loved you for years and years and years. And I will love you until I draw my dying breath."

He said nothing else, but pulled her closer. His arms came around her and she didn't deny him, but leaned in as he kissed her, this time with the love they felt out in the open. It was the most glorious kiss of her lifetime, soft at first, then asking for more, taking more, merging them in some way that was more than physical.

And yet as much joy as that gave her, it didn't wash away the hesitations that had kept her from reaching for this connection in the first place.

"What if loving each other isn't enough?" she asked. "The barriers are still there. I don't want to be seen as grabbing for power by involving myself in yet another part of it."

"Grantham already said what I know to be true. No one in the world could ever compare you to Alistair. Will people be suspect of what Grantham intends to build? Probably at first, but it will have nothing to do with you. But as they see their impact on their own futures grow, as he does what he has promised and makes this not a nation ruled by one but one ruled by all, they will not question him. And that is up to *him* to create, helped by all of us."

She bent her head. He wasn't wrong. "I suppose I could make it clear I was not involved in government by creating a charitable society. Expand on the one we saw in Bellsport. Dedicate my life to helping, not ruling."

"I agree," he said. "And if that still feels not enough, then we could marry."

She blinked up at him. "Marry?"

"Yes," he said slowly. "If you love me as I love you, if we are talking about a future together, I could not be fully happy unless you were my wife. Please tell me you would want the same."

"God, I have never felt free enough to even consider that option," she said. "A marriage that I chose, to a man I adore. Something that isn't for political gain or purpose, but only because we wish to live the rest of our lives together. Oh, Dash, I would very much like that."

"So you are saying yes?"

"If you are asking me."

He laughed. "Marry me. Please marry me. Be my partner and my friend and my very passionate lover for the rest of my life. Warm my life and give it purpose, as you have been doing for over ten years. Love me. And know that I will love you with all the ferocity in myself."

"I already do know that," she whispered. "And yes, yes I would marry you."

He dropped his mouth back to hers and kissed her once again. Her fears, though not entirely erased, were eased by his certainty. Her future, which had seemed so foggy, now felt clear. And for the first time in her life, Giabella knew that she was choosing a path that would be her joy until the end of her days.

And that felt like a very happily ever after, indeed.

EPILOGUE

Three months later

Giabella looked over the swirling ballroom from the balcony above it and breathed in a sigh of pleasure. Grantham was welcoming dignitaries from all over the world for his first fete as prime minister, and it couldn't have gone better. She watched him dance with Ophelia and saw the joy on his face. The certainty that made him all the better as a leader and man and, if she had understood the whispering that was getting louder each day, very soon a father.

Her gaze slipped to Remi and Priscilla. They were standing along the wall together, him bracing an arm beside her head, her looking up at him with adoration and love. He had taken up a strong position working beside Marabelle the last six months, the siblings becoming a voice for the people and their needs. He had purpose and love and happiness unlike anything she'd seen in his life before.

She found Sasha next. She and Thomas were standing with Count Friskar. Sasha leaned forward, talking to the man as Thomas beamed at her. She had become so much more joyful and at ease with herself as countess. Where she had once not known her place in the world, now it was clear.

Ilaria was last, laughingly balancing a plate of finger food on her pregnant belly as Jonah shook his head in playful judgment. Jonah had recently run for a position in the House of Commons in England and won. He was surrendering his title as Count in Athawick during this trip, and he seemed pleased with it.

Giabella felt arms come around her from behind and glanced back to smile as Dash cradled her against him. "Looking in on the children, I see," he said, kissing her neck and lighting her up the way he always could.

"Just thinking that when we all piled onto the ship with thoughts of arranging a political marriage for Ilaria in England, I never could have imagined how much would change for my children. For our country." She turned into Dash's arms and lifted herself up to kiss his lips. "For me."

"And for me," he said.

She nodded. Dash had taken his role as minister of the interior after the election and was often lauded for his understanding of Athawick's needs. He also took time to help her with her charitable society when he could. She had adopted the cause of orphans in Athawick and found it the most satisfying work she'd ever done. And despite all her fears, no one had ever said anything about her having undue influence on either her son or her husband.

"To think I almost let all this go," she said with a shiver. "How much I would have lost."

"But you didn't," he said, cupping her chin. "You didn't lose. Neither did they. Somehow we did the impossible. We all won." He kissed her again and parted with a groan. "As much as I would like to do that all night long, perhaps we should go back to the party."

She threaded her fingers through his. "Lead the way, my love."

He turned back, one brow arched. "No, not lead. Where we go, we go together, and we always shall."

"Always," she agreed as they came to the stairs that would take them back to their lives, their family and their happiness that seemed to have no bounds.

~

100 NIGHTS WITH THE DUKE

He moved toward the tea set on the sideboard and was about to pour himself a cup when the door opened once more. But this time it wasn't a servant. At last, Sophia, herself, stepped inside.

Edward sucked in a breath. God's teeth but she was beautiful, with thick, black hair, high cheekbones and impossibly bright blue eyes. There had likely never been a man who had stood in her presence who hadn't been enchanted by her beauty.

And yet there was so much more to how he felt when he looked at her. He saw the bright intelligence in her stare, the confidence in the way she moved, the sensuality in the twitch of her hips. There had never been another woman in his life who had enchanted him so utterly and completely. And even after all this time, that remained an immovable fact.

"Your Grace," she said as she stepped into the room. She hesitated before she reached back and shut the door, giving them privacy.

"So formal," he managed to choke out when he could form cogent words.

She swallowed hard before she responded. "I…I think it's best."

So she said, but he saw her gaze slide to his lips and then back up again. The expression belied her statement and his mouth burned like she had actually touched him there.

"Is it?" he pressed and moved a step closer. "Even after last night?"

Her mouth fluttered ever so slightly. "I—last night was a mistake, Your Grace. A weakness."

"One we share." He stepped toward her again, but this time she stiffened and he forced himself to stop. He couldn't push this too far or too hard. He knew that. He knew her.

And in truth, he owed her more than seduction, didn't he? So much more.

"Sophia, you cannot know how much I have missed you. How much I have thought of you over these past few years."

There, now the words were out. Only she didn't smile or preen or move toward him. Instead she backed away. "How very unfair to your late wife."

He flinched. "No truer words have ever been spoken. It was. I have hated myself for that a very long time, I assure you. Hated myself for that. And for how I treated you."

She held his gaze evenly but didn't offer him respite with words. She didn't try to make him more comfortable. But then again, he hadn't earned that.

He drew very deep breath. "Sophia, I'm sorry. Those are incredibly empty words, but they must be said before I can make any attempt to prove them. I'm so very sorry about what happened all those years ago. About what I did. What I didn't do."

She blinked up at him. "You…you needn't be, Edward."

He drank in how she said his given name. That was a softening, he knew. And he couldn't help but recall how she had moaned it in the past as she arched beneath him. He pushed the intrusive thought away and refocused. "We both know that isn't true," he replied. "Sorry is not a strong enough word for what I *need* to be as I stand here before you."

She shook her head. "You are a duke. You were required to marry a lady. You were a decent enough man that you didn't want to betray your wife with a mistress—"

"But as you said, I did betray her by always thinking of you."

She dropped her gaze. "That is unfortunate, but I'm not the one who requires an apology for it. You must know I don't—I don't hate you for it. I never did, even if I wished I could."

He sighed. "But I hurt you."

She didn't deny it, but paced away. "Everyone got hurt, it seems." She kept her gaze out the window for a moment, then turned back. "Why—why are you here? Why were you there last night?"

He smoothed his hands along the front of his waistcoat and took a deep breath. Here was the tricky part. He couldn't push too hard or too fast or she would run. He couldn't demand because it wasn't fair to her. He had to follow his very carefully laid plans, the ones that would act as apology, the ones that would show her his love.

"I told you, Sophia, I have not stopped thinking about you over the years. Since my mourning period is over now, I needed to see you. I wanted to…to be with you."

Her eyes went wide and a shiver moved through her that gave him further hope. "Edward…" she began, her tone wary and her expression poised for rejection.

He stepped toward her, closing the lion's share of the distance now in a long stride. "Please, Sophia. Answer me one question and then we can debate the rest. Have you thought of me over the years?"

The Duke of Hearts

The Duke Who Lied

The Duke of Desire

The Last Duke

The Scandal Sheet

The Return of Lady Jane

Stealing the Duke

Lady No Says Yes

My Fair Viscount

Guarding the Countess

The House of Pleasure

Seasons

An Affair in Winter

A Spring Deception

One Summer of Surrender

Adored in Autumn

The Wicked Woodleys

Forbidden

Deceived

Tempted

Ruined

Seduced

Fascinated

To see a complete listing of Jess Michaels' titles, please visit:

http://www.authorjessmichaels.com/books

ABOUT THE AUTHOR

USA Today Bestselling author Jess Michaels likes geeky stuff, Vanilla Coke Zero, anything coconut, cheese and her dog, Elton. She is lucky enough to be married to her favorite person in the world and lives in the heart of Dallas, TX where she's trying to eat all the amazing food in the city.

When she's not obsessively checking her steps on Fitbit or trying out new flavors of Greek yogurt, she writes historical romances with smoking hot characters and emotional stories. She has written for numerous publishers and is now fully indie and loving every moment of it (well, almost every moment).

Jess loves to hear from fans! So please feel free to contact her at Jess@AuthorJessMichaels.com.

Jess Michaels offers a free book to members of her newsletter, so sign up on her website:
http://www.AuthorJessMichaels.com/

facebook.com/JessMichaelsBks

twitter.com/JessMichaelsBks

instagram.com/JessMichaelsBks

bookbub.com/authors/jess-michaels

www.ingramcontent.com/pod-product-compliance
Lightning Source LLC
Chambersburg PA
CBHW030839200726

48285CB00007B/2485